Somebody Doesn't Like

Sarah Leigh

By **Peg Herring**

Gwendolyn Press

Somebody Doesn't Like Sarah Leigh

© Peg Herring, 2011, 2015

Printed in the USA

Cover Art: yocladesigns (http://yocladesigns.com)

Gwendolyn Press
ISBN 978-0-9861475-5-5

Chapter One

I couldn't see the terrified woman behind me in the dark woods, but I heard her labored breathing, almost synchronized with my own. Frequently we stumbled into trees, gasped in pain at the lash of a branch across the face, and stubbed our toes on unseen rocks and roots. I sensed her flagging energy, but I wasn't much better off. And, I asked myself angrily, why should I care if she fell behind?

We had to stop running soon. We had pushed ourselves farther than I'd have thought possible for two women almost into the fifth decade of life. In addition, we made so much noise crashing through the woods like crazed hippos that tracking us was easy for our pursuers. Worst of all, we had no idea where we were going. We might end up making a big circle and coming face to face with the very people we were trying desperately to avoid.

Sensing something in my path, I stopped. The way ahead was blocked by a tree broken off halfway up, no doubt by lightning. Its jagged trunk pointed into the sky, but its branches swept the ground, held in place by a splinter of raw white wood that caught what little moonlight there was.

Unable to see that I'd stopped, my companion plunged

into me. Her push sent me forward a step, and I caught my balance by grasping the branches that swept the ground before me. As I did, my foot felt the edge of a depression. The ruined tree's top lay over a gully, and its thick branches hid the space beneath. A place we might rest and evade capture? It was better than nothing.

In low tones I communicated what I had in mind. The dim form beside me offered no objection. Navigating my way through the branches and into the hole, I held them aside so she could crawl in as well. The space, just wide enough for the two of us to curl into, was half-filled with leaves fast turning to compost, but the surrounding depth felt protective. We lay there, struggling to quiet our exhausted lungs and staring into the darkness as if by sheer will we could see danger approaching.

In minutes, we heard them. One was some distance off but noisy. The nearer one was stealthy, pausing every few steps to listen. When he stopped beside us, I could have reached out and touched the fluorescent stripe on his sneaker.

Each second's passing seemed to shave a year off my life. It was terrifying to lie there imagining what would happen if they found us. The two men had planned we'd die by fire, but no doubt they'd come up with a Plan B to cover this situation. If we died out here, would anyone find our bodies? Not for years. Our only hope of staying alive was complete silence.

"They're here somewhere," the noisy one called.

"Sh-h-h!" hissed the other, the words barely a sound.

The men stood for a long time, waiting for us to betray ourselves with a movement, cough, or cry. They say it's impossible for two women to keep silent for long, but neither of us so much as twitched. While my body remained tense and still, my mind worked overtime.

How had this happened to me? The fact that I was hiding from murderers, desperate men who intended I would breathe my last before this night was over, was due to a woman who'd once been such a close friend I could never have imagined she'd turn on me. Because of her I'd suffered confusion and stress, told the biggest lie of my life, was suspect in a mysterious disappearance, and was now a candidate for murder victim. As we sat frozen, our legs cramping in that earthy almost-grave, I had a long time to consider my situation. What had I done to deserve this? Until two years ago, I'd been Sarah Elizabeth Leigh's best friend.

Chapter Two

I'd known Sarah Mathews Leigh since before I could remember. We were the same age—actually, she was four months older, which she used to mention often when we were kids but stopped noting when we hit twenty. Our mothers went to the same church, sang in the same choir, taught Sunday school together, and played bridge on Friday nights. Sarah and I played together as babies. I don't remember a time when she wasn't around.

I grew up comparing myself to Sarah, who was demure where I was brash, circumspect where I was impulsive, and tactful where I was (am) inclined to be impatient. Sarah never seemed to mind the things that drive me crazy: mindless tasks, waiting around, and the inefficiency of the clueless.

I remember once suggesting to our Sunday school teacher that she might not have so many problems with the Stickley brothers if she planned activities that were a little more interesting. Her lips tightened just like when the boys were at their worst, and she said in that quavery, high-pitched voice that begged to be mimicked, "You should try to be more like Sarah, Caroline. She doesn't criticize her elders *or* laugh when those boys act up."

It was true. Sarah never caused the slightest irritation for the adults we encountered, and even my own mother sometimes held her up as a shining example. "Margaret Mathews never has a minute's trouble with that girl," she'd say. She never added out loud what I knew she was thinking: "Why can't you be more like Sarah?"

Both our mothers are gone now, but if I could see mine once more, the question I'd ask is not what heaven is like or how it feels to die. I'd ask if her friend Margaret Mathews ever made her as furious, as downright hysterical, as her daughter Sarah eventually made me.

They say people grow apart sometimes. All I can say is that in our case, we didn't just grow apart. One of us grew malicious.

It was cold in the damp hole, and I pressed my lips together to stop my teeth from chattering. I hadn't come dressed for a March night in Michigan's north woods. My loafers were soaked, my jeans felt clammy in the seat from the rotting leaves beneath me, and the scratches on my arms and face burned. I was a mess.

Another memory came to mind: our prissy neighbor Mrs. Albine, who from time to time took it upon herself to scold me for being such a tomboy. "Look at your little friend," she'd urge. "Such a little lady! If you took the time in the morning to braid your hair like Sarah's, it wouldn't fly all over." When my hair hadn't displeased her it was the dirt on my knees, the hole in my sleeve, or the scratches I'd earned climbing into blackberry bushes. I wondered what the old biddy would think if she could see me now.

Sometimes the dark is a woman's friend.

Chapter Three

Sarah and I were close growing up, despite our differences. In high school we shared clothes, lipsticks, and boyfriends with equal lack of concern. I should state that in those days boyfriends were just that: boys who were friends. Sarah and I dated twins for a while, but neither of us paid much attention to which of them kissed us goodnight. It was all perfectly innocent.

After graduation we were separated for a while. Sarah, whose parents had little money and few aspirations for their children, went to beauty school, while I trained to be an RN. Back then that meant leaving northern Michigan, but when I graduated, I returned home. Sarah had married (I was maid of honor) and already had a small child. She'd set up shop with two other women and seemed content with her choices. We took up our friendship again as easily as putting on an often-washed flannel shirt.

Abaletta is a small town in northern Lower Michigan, usually located for strangers by pointing to a spot on the inside of your index finger, near the first knuckle. The northeastern side of Michigan's "mitten" is sometimes considered less blessed by Mother Nature. The long-ago glaciers left more of an impression on the western side, giving rise to places like Traverse City and Petoskey, where lovely hills sweep down to charming bays. Tourists flock to the west side to enjoy the views, the sports, and the waters.

East of I-75 the land is flatter, the coastline less impressive. There are fewer vacationers, more long-established families and retirees from the auto plants of Detroit. Abaletta is inland from the Great Lakes, just a dot on the way to Lake Huron. Our only housing development is the trailer park, and fast food consists of a ham and cheese at the gas station's deli counter.

Although there are no ski hills on the Sunrise Side, there is peace and quiet. There's plenty of recreational water too: lakes of all sizes, rivers, and the only waterfall in the Lower Peninsula (Ocqueoc Falls, which is pronounced AH-kee-ahk. The name brings endless delight to locals who love to hear tourists try to say it correctly). I never wanted to live anywhere else, despite the fact there's only one stoplight—in the whole county.

I married shortly after getting my nurses' cap, and when Sarah's James was almost two, Ben and I had our first child. We babysat for each other, joined committees together hoping to expand the insular world of Abaletta, and generally enjoyed each other's company. We held the same political and social views, pretty much middle-of-the-road on everything. Over the years we cooperated on local events, worked the concession stand at the school, and even shared the chairpersonship of the local Friends of the Library. The first thought either of us had when something happened, good or bad, was to call the other and tell her.

Sarah was the quiet one, and her face lit up when she saw me in a way that almost made me feel guilty sometimes, like I was someone special. There wasn't much fun in Sarah's life outside the time she and I spent on our various projects. Her husband, though not a bad person, was the so-called "man's man" who didn't share much of his time with his wife. Sarah seldom talked about their relationship, even with me, but what slipped out from time to time made me feel sorry for her. Once I was babbling about Ben and his foibles Sarah asked, "Does Ben ever tell you he loves you?"

"Not every ten minutes, like some people," I replied. "He usually sings it, slightly off-key, with the likes of Jim Croce or Rod Stewart."

"Marv won't say it." She stared straight ahead as she spoke. "I even asked him to once, but he won't."

I didn't have a good response, but I tried. "He loves you,

Sarah," I told her. "He married you."

"I was pregnant."

"Oh." She'd never mentioned it, but of course I can count. "Just the same, he loves you. I can tell."

That was pure bunk, because I didn't know Marv well at all, despite our growing up in the same town. Marvin Leigh was a standout in high school, but he hadn't run with our crowd. In fact, Marv's friends were the type for whom dedication to a cause meant ramming your head into your locker door to psych up for a football game.

Marv and Sarah's relationship began during baseball/softball season our senior year, a direct result of the fact that the two teams shared a bus for away games. Softball was the one thing in high school that Sarah did without me, and she was really good. When she and Marv started dating a lot of people were surprised, but Sarah is pretty in a quiet way, and she was a definite step up from his previous girlfriends.

Like most females our age, we'd grown up with "Don't," "You can't," and "What will people think?" It's hard to leave that well-meant litany behind, but we stuck together, two "good" girls viewed with grudging admiration by our peers. When I went away to school, Sarah had no one to hang onto but Marv, and their relationship gelled. I hoped that Sarah would make Marvin Leigh into the man he was capable of becoming.

Though Sarah's parents were thrilled she'd caught the eye of the local football star, I'd never thought much of their judgment. Mrs. Mathews was the kind who puts the *just* in "just a housewife": no hobbies, no talents, no interests outside the home, and even what was there was dull as dishwater.

Sarah's dad thought Marv was great, but I suspected that was partly relief that their marriage ended any silly thoughts Sarah might have had of going on to higher education. If she'd done that, he might have been expected to make some sort of financial contribution, and Bob Mathews was the type who saw college as a waste of time, especially for females. He probably thought of Marv as the best thing for Sarah, a practical man who'd keep her feet on the ground and her head out of the clouds.

To be truthful, I found Marv slightly greasy, the kind of man whose gaze is a foot too low when he talks to a woman. Still, he was a decent provider, and some of the locals lauded his business acumen. I told myself you don't have to like your best friend's mate. You just smile a lot and say nothing.

Sarah seemed convinced that Marv was everything a man should be. Sometimes I could manage only a noncommittal, "Mmm," when she hinted that other men cowered in Marv's presence while women swooned at his feet. Many in town declared them a mismatched couple, but that's an old story, from Heathcliff and Kathy to made-for-TV weepers. They'd made it work for them, and that was all that mattered.

Sometimes a weak marriage is strengthened by the children, but here again, Sarah had some trials. Sarah's older son, Jason, was a nice kid but so quiet it was hard to remember he was there. Two days after graduating high school, he left Abaletta and never returned. Sarah had never met her daughter-in-law and grandson. "Marv doesn't like to travel," she'd explain. Jason didn't seem interested in it either.

The second son, James, was a more active problem. After living at home until he was twenty-five, he moved in with a succession of low-class, hard-living women who shared his streak of aggression. These temporary pairings often led to loud, violent quarrels requiring police intervention. James was uncommunicative and surly when sober, but when he drank, he was a real handful. Everyone in town felt sorry for Sarah, and most blamed James' behavior on Marv's side of the family. "Sarah's such a sweetheart," they'd say. "It's a shame that boy turned out so much like his grandfather, old Jake Leigh."

Maybe because of her own troubles, Sarah looked to me as a shining example. Mostly through luck (since choices we make in our twenties seldom stem from any sort of deep wisdom), I married happily and raised two children who did well, though the town whispered it was past time one of them gave me grandchildren.

Back when we were more than just civil to each other, Sarah often asked about my kids, apparently enjoying stories of their adventures in the wider world. She seldom talked about her boys, and when she did it seemed carefully measured, as if she decided what had to be told and then made it as palatable as possible. "Jason got a promotion at work. He's very happy, but it means he can't come home for the Fourth again this year."

Then she'd ask about Rachel or Tony, and I'd tell the latest funny or interesting things they'd been doing, hamming it up until she giggled at my antics.

My life changed abruptly one day when my beloved Ben came home from work, said he didn't feel well, and died of a massive coronary only a few minutes later. For a year afterward I was lost in grief, self-absorbed, surly, and unwilling to participate in life, as if I could punish it for hurting me.

Such events bring out the best in towns and in friendships. Everyone in Abaletta went out of their way to let me know how saddened they were by Ben's death and my loneliness. And gradually my friend Sarah, without shaming or blaming, encouraged me to go out in public again, to take up my old duties in civic affairs and to mix with people.

Being a widow is like anything else; no one is good at it right away. It takes practice, guts, and time to begin again and build a different sort of life. I was grateful to have Sarah beside me those first few times I faced my friends and neighbors without Ben. I learned to tolerate their pity, and gradually they stopped thinking of me as "Poor Caroline." I became just Caroline again.

My children were supportive, though Tony, an airline pilot, spends a lot of time literally *over* seas. To him I'm just Mom, and the possibility that I could fall apart never occurred to him. Tony calls once a month and texts from time to time, but mostly he just thinks of me fondly. On the other hand, Rachel sensed how altered my life was without Ben and made an effort to speak with me several times a week, giving me little pep talks I didn't think I needed but did.

Despite the fact that life didn't turn out the way I'd planned, I had my children to sustain me. And despite the fact that her life wasn't idyllic, Sarah had someone to hold onto as well: a grand-daughter I hoped made up for her other disappointments.

In one of his tumultuous relationships, James had fathered a child with a woman who, once she was a mother, rejected parenthood out of hand. She moved on—to Oklahoma, I heard—and James was left a single father of doubtful qualification. Sarah poured her affection onto the child, a little girl whimsically named Spring, and spent as much time with her as possible. Sarah's love for Spring had to be rewarding, and it was obvious to everyone who saw them together that the child adored Nana Leigh.

That was my life in Abaletta until two years ago, give or take a month. Sarah and I were friends, and when we were working on something or dallying over lunch, the differences in our lives didn't matter, at least to me. If Sarah wasn't ecstatically happy in her marriage, I admired her for holding her head up and building on the other areas of life: church, civic, and social. If her children were a disappointment in some ways, I told myself there were compensations in others.

***

The moon showed for a few minutes, wisps of cloud racing past it like they were in a hurry to get somewhere. I was glad when it disappeared again. Dark was what we needed, though it felt like all the lights in the world had gone out. We were alone, and we were not alone, safe yet not. I wished I were somewhere else, anywhere else.

***

"I wish I were somewhere else." For no apparent reason, my mind dredged up a comment made by Sarah's son Jason one day years ago when I'd given him a ride home from football practice. He'd been about fourteen then, gangly, uncoordinated, and shy.

"What do you mean, Jason?"

The boy's earnest eyes sought mine in the rearview mirror, something that seldom occurred. Well-behaved, polite, and difficult to know, Jason spoke little and revealed almost nothing of what went on in his head. His grades were good, the opposite of his brother James', but he made himself almost invisible by being mostly silent and totally unremarkable.

"I hate football."

I kept my tone non-judgmental. "Why's that, Jase?"

Thin shoulders rose and fell. "It's dumb."

"You don't have to play."

There was a pause. "Dad thinks I do."

"Oh." Neither of Marv's sons was destined to equal his glory days. Jason's performance was lackluster, and James never came close to being eligible, even if he'd any inclination to do as his father wished.

I'd felt a stab of pity for Jason, trying to please his dad when he'd never be anything but second string. I wondered if Marv gave the kid any credit at all for trying, or if only superstar status would satisfy him.

Marv often commented on our Tony's football prowess, never caring if his sons were within hearing. "Now there's a boy to be proud of," he'd say, and I'd see Ben glance at the Leigh boys to judge how they took the implied criticism. It was no wonder Jason had wished he were someplace else, no wonder he'd gone there as soon as he was able.

Maybe I too should have moved far away from Sarah and Marv Leigh, I thought. Maybe I'd have been better off.

The clouds above us thickened, blotting out the moon entirely.

Chapter Four

My first clue things were going sour between Sarah and me came one afternoon at lunch. A group of ten of us had a standing date one Saturday a month for whoever could make it. It was a chance to catch up on each other's lives, gossip, and be girls again, forgetting the responsibilities of adulthood. I'd guess the wait staff hated to see us coming. We were noisy and often silly, and we always stretched a salad and an iced tea into a two-hour confab.

At this particular lunch there were seven of us, and I told a story of how an irritating woman had made everything about her first-visit paperwork ten times harder than it had to be. As the rest of them laughed, I noted an angry expression on Sarah's face. That was unusual, and I made a mental note to ask in private if there was something wrong at home. For the rest of the lunch Sarah avoided looking at me, turning her body away and speaking only to those on her other side. After a while, it was downright ridiculous.

When we left I caught up with her as she strode toward her van. "Hey, wait up!" She turned, no sign of welcome on her face. "Sarah, is something wrong?"

"No." Her body language screamed the opposite.

"You acted a little funny in there." I had a thought; sometimes I'm a little slow. "Did I say something wrong?"

"You made fun of the woman at the clinic."

I hadn't identified the woman by name, just described what happened, admittedly with sarcastic asides. Sarcasm is part of my charm—I think. "Well, it was pretty irritating," I defended myself. "Her insisting we justify every single question on the form."

"Maybe she was concerned."

"I'm sure she was, but we have other things to do."

"Right. You're busy with your career."

I frowned. "Look, Sarah, I admit I made fun of the woman, but she wasn't there. She'll never know."

"What you won't say to someone's face, you shouldn't say at all."

Now I was totally lost. I've never claimed to be as good a person as Sarah, who never gossips. But she'd been my friend forever and knew perfectly well I'm a bit—maybe a lot—impatient with people who waste my time. She'd never indicated it was a problem before. Mumbling a feeble farewell, I promised to see her the next day. She didn't even answer me. On the drive home, I decided Sarah must somehow have identified with the lady I'd groused about.

The next time I noticed something wrong was at a PTA meeting. Jan Chambers, the chair, asked if anyone had ideas for a fundraiser. I suggested a Men's Beauty Pageant, a gag thing where lunch would be served and the guys would parody the whole pageant thing with funny swimsuits, awful talent, and lots of strutting.

Jan fell in with the suggestion immediately. "Do you think they'd wear evening gowns?"

"Oh, that would be good," another woman said with a chuckle.

"And heels," chimed in a third. Soon ideas were flying thick and fast. Corny, I know, but popular.

With a tiny wave of her hand, Sarah Leigh intervened. "Won't that upset the Miss Abaletta committee? They've worked hard to build a good reputation for their pageant. Should we make fun of it?"

A few tried to say it was all in good fun, but Sarah plainly saw no merit in it. In the face of her disapproval, the idea died. I didn't argue, but I had the feeling she didn't dislike the idea of a mock pageant as much as she disliked my coming up with it.

After that I noticed more and more animosity. For years I'd been the leader and Sarah the backup. That didn't mean she was less important, but I'm naturally more outgoing (mouthy, some might say). Sarah liked working in the background, or so I thought. She simply didn't have the assertiveness (pushiness?) it takes to chair a meeting or create an event.

I never thought less of her for it. In fact I appreciated Sarah for keeping me rooted in practicality. Someone would ask, "Caroline, will you head up the drive for the Humane Society this year?" I'd be doubtful about taking one more thing on, but Sarah would pipe up, "I'll help, Caro," and it would be doable.

Sarah was real help too, not like some who make promises and later give lame excuses for not following through. She was there when she said she'd be, and I had always appreciated what she did. I listened to her opinions. I bragged about her when people commented she was timid and overly solemn. We were a team, and it worked.

Then it didn't work anymore. Sarah disagreed with me on almost everything, and not sweetly, as she once would have. Now there was anger that surprised me. "You can't do it that way!" she'd say, and her lips would pull in like closing doors. I usually backed down, but I could never figure out exactly what it was I'd done that was so wrong.

Sarah seemed irritated with anything I did. At meetings I chaired, she sat looking down at her knees. When the others were gone, she challenged what I'd said, her objections picayune and caustic. Why was my friend so unhappy with me?

Oddly, everyone else saw the sweet, smiling Sarah they'd always seen. Only for me did the smile on her lips never make it to her eyes. Sarah seemed able to tolerate everyone in town except the person who was supposed to be her best friend.

I tried asking others if they noticed anything different. From most I got "Isn't she just the sweetest thing?" One friend commented, "I bet you feel lucky to have Sarah around."

I used to, I wanted to say, but I kept quiet.

One person had an interesting comment, but since he had nothing good to say about anyone, it hardly counted. When I asked Diane Gehring if Sarah seemed distracted, she said no, but her husband Jeff, standing a step back and half-turned away as usual, overheard and commented in his grumpy way, "Do you mean she's *distracted* as in not thinking about what she's doing, or *distract* in the

Shakespearean sense, out of her mind?"

I shouldn't have asked, because I hate his pedantic, superior manner, which is based on the fact that he teaches a few classes at the local junior college. Still, I wanted to know what other people saw in Sarah. "Which one fits?"

He raised skinny eyebrows over deep-set, shiny-black eyes. "Both, I'd say. The woman's a classic enabler who lets that husband of hers get away with all kinds of shenanigans."

"Sarah's just kind-hearted." Diane warned her husband into silence with her eyes. "Caroline of all people knows that." She chuckled. "Now, I hear you've caught the interest of a certain bachelor in town."

"I don't know what you're talking about."

Diane's smile turned arch. "He asked about you."

"He who?"

Jeff nudged his wife with more than usual irritation. "Come on, Woman. We've got seed to buy."

Diane gave me an I'll-talk-with-you-later look and hurried off after the Grouch. I went on, feeling disgusted. Instead of finding out the answer to my little mystery, I had another one to puzzle on. What man in Abaletta had been dumb enough to show interest in me out loud? The gossips would have us married before I even learned his identity.

So that was it. Everyone agreed Sarah's only fault was being too kind to dump her awful husband and give the boot to her useless son. In the end, I told the whole story to the only person I could really talk to about it, my daughter Rachel. She suggested I simply come out and ask Sarah what the problem was.

"I've tried," I insisted, building a ketchup sandwich as we chatted. "Several times I've gotten her alone so she has the chance to tell me what's bothering her. She won't say anything."

"She's waiting for an opening from you, Mom. All these years you've been the leader."

"I've come as close as I can to demanding an explanation." I will admit that I avoid asking questions when I'm afraid the answer might upset me. "Yesterday I said, 'Sarah, is there something we should talk about?' and then I looked right at her."

"That was fairly direct, for you." Rachel sounded amused.

"It didn't help. All she said was, 'No, Caroline, I don't think so.' Then she walked away."

Knowing my attempt seemed feeble to my assertiveness-trained eldest, I tried to rationalize. "It's a small town, Rachel. There's no sense in having a knock-down, drag-out fight with someone you're going to see every day for the rest of your life."

"So you'll go on pretending things are okay?"

"It's better than starting a squabble that will have everyone in town taking sides."

"I just hate the idea of this dragging on," Rachel countered. "It could be a misunderstanding."

I murmured something noncommittal, but I knew differently. Sarah's animosity wasn't a petty snit. A major change in her outlook had caused her to regard me as an enemy.

So it went on, like a nightmare where I was back in junior high, snubbed, criticized, and uneasy whenever a certain person was around. The worst of it was that that person was Sarah.

Anyone present at the meeting where she moved that Alison be team leader for Diet & Dance, our exercise group, would have seen nothing wrong. Only I knew Sarah finds Alison arrogant, and she'd admitted that only when I asked her point blank the year before.

So why did she suggest Alison? To avoid my being chosen. While I had no regrets about heading up one less organization, I wondered for the hundredth time what I'd done to earn the dislike of my best friend.

Chapter Five

Life goes on, of course. I had my family and my work to focus on, and that kept me busy. One day an elderly patient, Mrs. Bale, came into the clinic with disturbing symptoms. She needed tests we couldn't do, and that meant a drive to Petoskey. Doc didn't want her to drive herself, and my shift was about to end. Having once been a student in her class, I volunteered to take her.

Even at almost ninety Mrs. Bale was lively company,. She'd been a schoolteacher for years, and I was amazed to find she remembered not only her students from long ago but also their spouses and the names of most of their children. I learned a lot about quilting and flowers on the forty-minute drive, and that was fair recompense, because when I retire, I plan to have a garden as good as any in town.

I knew enough to expect that the trip would be at a snail's pace. Between Alanson and Petoskey, there's nowhere to pass and always someone determined to lead a parade of cars at forty miles an hour. As we turtled along, I asked Mrs. Bale about her recent knee replacement surgery. "Were you in the hospital long?"

"You know they don't keep you but five minutes after the

anesthetic wears off these days," she said with a chuckle. "My niece stayed at the house for a few days, and after that different people stopped by. Your friend Sarah was one."

"She's really good about that." I shook my head ruefully. "I'm always afraid I'll be intruding."

Mrs. Bale was silent, and I stole a glance at her. Was she thinking I was selfish, too busy with my own affairs to take time for others? Was she remembering me as a sixth-grader, skimming ahead because I simply couldn't wait for the other students to finish reading the assigned story? She probably thought I'd never grown up, never got over being a flibbertigibbet.

"To tell you the truth, I don't care much for duty visits," she said after a few moments.

"What do you mean?"

She frowned out the sunny front window. "I appreciate your friend's intentions, and I'm not criticizing her doing what she believes is kind. But nothing makes me feel more like a useless old person than having someone sit for two hours making pointless conversation because they think I need cheering up." She chuckled dryly. "I almost go crazy trying to come up with things to talk about."

I was surprised, but I shouldn't have been. Mrs. Bale,

sharp despite her aging body, recognized the patronizing aspect in the assumption she'd lost the ability to entertain herself.

We passed through Bay View, my favorite part of the trip. Founded by the Methodist Church in 1875 "for intellectual and scientific culture and the promotion of the cause of religion and morality," it's a community where century-plus-old homes line the road, lovingly kept and charmingly decorated with gingerbread. Some have striking colors, purples, greens, and pinks with improbable accent tones, while others opt for traditional white with bright-colored shutters or pennants on the porch for contrast. The place has a Gatsby-like feel to it, and the residents buy into the fiction, wearing white outfits to the tennis court on the lakeshore and biking the pathways with their expensive dogs for company.

As we registered at the clinic, I noticed a boy sitting on a gurney in the hallway. I'd met him several times when I worked in the ER here. He was half of an adventurous set of twins named Barr, and what one lad didn't think of, the other did. As a result, one or both of them was in the ER several times a year.

"What is it this time?" I asked, glancing at the leg wrapped in a bloodied towel. "And are you Tim or Tom?"

The twin who was unhurt (this time) came up behind me, a can of soda in either had, and answered for him. "That's Tom, and we were jumping our bikes. We found this cool pile of old snow fence, all rolled up and stacked just perfect."

Tom took up the story, his excitement undimmed by the bloody ending. "We laid some boards over it and started getting some really good air, but I misjudged my landing and caught the edge of a slat." Unwrapping the towel, he showed me his wound, a nasty gash in the fleshy part of his calf. He looked down at it clinically. "Six stitches, I bet."

Tim bent to make his own prognosis. "They'll sew that up in no time," he pronounced solemnly, and Tom nodded agreement.

"Can't you guys just ride your bikes normally?"

"Our way's more fun." Tim nodded in tacit support of his brother's words. A nurse arrived, and Tom was rolled away to the exam room. Tim went along, apparently eager to observe the repairs.

As I entered the waiting area, I saw the twins' mother slumped in a chair in reception. I remembered her first name was Angie. We'd made casual conversation during emergency visits enough times to consider ourselves acquaintances.

Angie, a pretty but tough-looking woman, apparently found men appealing only in the short term. While she'd been married to the boys' father, Mr. Barr, I had met at least three live-ins since they divorced. They'd been without exception sullen, gruff men who gravitated to Angie's hard beauty but probably didn't appreciate the lively set of twins that came with the package. She frowned into the pages of a paperback book, and when Mrs. Bale left with a nurse, I went over and sat down near her.

"Hi, Angie, remember me?"

She took a minute to focus. "Oh, hi. You work here, right?"

"Not anymore. I just brought in a patient."

Angie's smile was grim. "Me too." She pushed overlong bangs out of her eyes. "Blue Cross should give me a rebate for all the business I bring this place. Thank god it hasn't been anything terrible yet, but those two!" She rolled her eyes theatrically, more irritated with her sons than worried.

Not for the first time, I wondered where Angie was when her kids were off getting hurt. She obviously wasn't focused on watching them. I guessed she was focused on herself.

Tiny and intense, Angie was all air-brushed fingernails, highlighted hair, and makeup. The boys were probably more than she could handle, but she was philosophical, even blasé, about their antics. "Once Tim dared Tom to jump out a second-story window, and he did it. By some miracle he wasn't hurt, but he turned around and insisted Tim do it too. He ended up with a broken arm."

"I remember that one," I said with a chuckle.

"My brother was like that too. Always doing dumb stuff. It looks like the twins got his crazy streak." Shivering, she glanced out the window. "I hope they don't end up like him."

Rather than commenting on the unknown uncle's shenanigans, I merely nodded.

"The upside is that Tim's decided he wants to be a doctor, so he'll hold his brother's hand. All I have to do is drive them home afterward." She grimaced comically. "I might as well give them the car keys. They couldn't do any worse behind the wheel than they do on those damned bikes."

"They definitely keep you busy."

"Lots of waiting." Angie gestured at the novel she'd laid in her lap. "I always keep a book in my purse."

"What are you reading?"

"Just a mystery novel." She held it up. "The author's name caught my interest, cuz it's the same as a guy I knew once. I don't think they're related, though. The guy I dated was barely literate."

I grimaced at her use of *date.* It's sad that kids like Tim and Tom often don't know from week to week which "date" will come out of the bedroom at breakfast time.

Regarding me in a way that said everything about me was being weighed and judged, Angie asked, "Did you retire early or something?"

"No, I work at a clinic in Abaletta now. That's east of here."

"I know where it is," she said, brightening. "My brother had a job once helping to clear a road into some property, and he found this old cabin near there. Pete claimed Chris—my boyfriend at the time—owned it, because it said REDMAN on the side."

"Redman," I murmured. That struck a chord of memory, but it was a faint one. "Redman?"

"Yeah. Someone had patched a hole in the cabin wall with one of those big old metal signs, an ad for Red Man chewing tobacco. That's where Pete got that it was Chris' place, the 'Red Man' property. He thought it was hilarious." Her tone indicated she hadn't found it that funny.

I'd seen that cabin and the sign, but I couldn't place it. "It's on a lake, right?"

"Yeah. He took us there once." Angie's face seemed younger as she remembered happier days. "I don't remember much except it was in the boonies and we had to take a boat."

"Lots of cabins off the beaten track around there."

"It was kind of fun at first," she recalled. "We drove to the lakeshore and packed the boat with all kinds of stuff: food, paper plates, blankets, games, and everything to spend a few nights in the great outdoors. But that cabin?" She shuddered. "It was pretty rustic."

"Did it belong to someone?"

"Some paper company. They bought the land for the lumbering rights."

"Did you stay there?"

Angie shook her head. "Not for long. Within fifteen minutes, Pete cut his finger to the bone trying to chop wood for a campfire. We had to get right back into the boat and head for an emergency room." She rolled her eyes. "Like I said, my boys take after their uncle."

I was trying to picture the cabin from the water. Which lake had we been on when we saw it? "I know I've seen that

Red Man sign on a cabin wall," I told her. "My husband and I used to canoe a lot."

"The place wasn't much then, and it's probably worse now."

"I don't know," I said with a shrug. "A quiet place on a remote lake could be a great little hideaway."

Angie's reaction to the casual statement startled me. She twitched in her chair, dropping the book, which slid to the floor, its place marker sliding out and drifting under her chair.

"What?" I said, confused.

Angie's lashes swept down over her eyes, masking them, and her lips pulled together like the doors of an assailed fortress. Picking up the novel, she stuck the slender cardboard bookmark inside it with no attempt to find her place. "I just remembered I'm supposed to get my hair done this afternoon. I'd better call and cancel."

I'd have sworn her hair had just been done. The tips of each strand were expertly tipped with blond that contrasted nicely with the dark-dyed overall color.

Just then Mrs. Bale emerged from the lab and stopped at the desk to sign papers. Rising, I said it had been nice seeing

Angie again, despite the circumstances. I was beginning to miss lunch, and my mind was already on the choice between Arby's and Burger King.

When we turned to go, Angie had come up behind me. She spoke offhandedly, but there was an undercurrent that belied the casual approach. "So you know where that cabin is?"

"Not for sure," I replied. "I haven't been out there in a while, and when I was, I didn't pay it much attention."

"Which lake is it on?"

I shrugged. "It could be any of a dozen."

There was a long pause, as if she wanted to continue but didn't know what approach to take. "I just wondered," she said finally.

"I hope things are okay with Tom," I said in parting.

"Yeah, thanks." I left, wondering how she could take so lightly her bleeding child in some hidden room beyond reception. But then again, Tim and Tom seemed used to operating without their mother's undivided attention.

Chapter Six

One of the complications in my life caused by Sarah's turning against me hadn't seemed to matter much at the time. In the year after Ben's death I'd felt an urgent need to do something different, perhaps to prove to myself that I was still alive. I wrote a book. Two news stories that developed in nearby towns had given me the idea of putting them together to make a mystery novel.

The only person I told about the book was Sarah. If I'd dared to call myself a writer in public, it would have been quite a joke in Abaletta. Still, I was sure my plot idea was good, if I could find the right words to tell it. I explained to Sarah that my writing was therapy, not the belief that I was the next Sara Paretsky.

Sarah waited eagerly to read each chapter as I finished. Since there's nothing more flattering than someone begging to see what you've written, I let her. She even helped with research, ferreting out details I needed to make the story realistic. Of course, I changed the facts around to suit the needs of my novel. I had no intention of writing true crime.

There were facts, of course. A person or persons unknown had taken advantage of the fact that the beautiful homes in Bay View sit empty from October to May. They'd robbed them in mid-winter, when most of the streets aren't even plowed.

Items taken were mostly art, jewelry, and expensive knick-knacks: antique cigarette cases, diamond-studded tiepins, that sort of thing. The police reported that electronics and other more practical items went untouched. The thefts were discovered only when a couple who'd come north for a ski weekend stopped by to check on their house and found things missing.

What intrigued me was the ease with which the thieves got into the houses. In most cases there was no sign of forcible entry. It appeared to be a series of inside jobs, but who had access to a dozen of the homes? Caterers, landscapers, and others who worked in the community were considered, but nothing came of it. The crimes stopped after that one winter. No one was ever arrested, and the goods were never found.

The second part of my story came from an accident that I turned into murder through author's privilege. A man's body was found in the woods several miles from Ridgely, a town about forty miles from Bay View. He'd been shot with a hunting rifle, and the theory was someone had been violating (the local term for poaching) and fired at what he thought was a deer. The shooter apparently panicked and ran when he realized he'd killed a man.

However, the incident was odd. The victim, a tavern owner, wore only a light jacket, no hat or boots despite the day's blustery wind and a few inches of snow on the ground. Maybe a "fudgie" (our term, for down-state vacationers because so many of them buy fudge) would go into the woods like that in early spring, but Peter Miltowski was a northern Michigan native who should have known better.

What was he doing so far from his house and his business? Some theorized he'd been with a woman and they'd had a fight, but his family knew of no such involvement. Besides, would there be a rifle handy for an angry girlfriend to pick up and use to kill Miltowski?

The police questioned certain locals well-known for hunting out of season and looked hard at Miltowski's life as well. Nothing proved it wasn't an accident; nothing proved it was. They might have suspected there was more to the story, but as time passed, no more information came to light.

My idea was to put the two crimes together. In my version, the dead man was one of a gang who burglarized homes in Bay View. Planning to double-cross his pals, he hid the stolen goods. Then, like so many criminals, he couldn't help but drop hints about how clever he'd been during a visit to a small hair salon. That clue for the book's detective was a tribute to my friend Sarah.

It might sound like a stretch to have a criminal brag that he'll be coming into a lot of money soon, but it's amazing what people tell their hairdressers. Like bartenders, listening is part of a cosmetologist's. Relaxed customers talk—and tell.

My detective figured things out from the details the victim told the stylist in his moment of gabbiness. That made the crimes solvable, and the rest was filling in chases, clues, and false leads to make the plot exciting. I started and stopped a lot, being new to novel writing, so it was sometimes months before a new chapter was added and a full year before the whole thing took shape.

The book almost got finished. I mean, the story itself was complete, but I'd planned to go back and fine-tune some of the characters and add at least one more subplot. I asked Sarah to read it again and pencil in ideas for improvement. I gave her the draft on CD, suggesting it was easier to make corrections on the computer, but she said she preferred a hard copy. To save her having to print the whole thing I gave her mine, with notes in the margin that asked, "More here?"

or "Does this sound phony?"

Months passed, and Sarah stopped mentioning the book. Her strange behavior toward me had begun, which made it awkward to ask. When I brought the topic up a few times, I got only vague responses. In the end I figured she was trying to spare my feelings. Somewhere I'd gone wrong with the story, and she was too embarrassed to tell me.

That winter I bought a new computer. In the process of clearing files from the old one, I deleted the manuscript, knowing I had saved it on a CD. Only after I'd done that did I remember Sarah had both the hard copy and the CD.

Since she'd been acting so funny, I didn't bring up what might be another sore subject. I had no confidence in my future as an author, and Sarah's avoidance of the topic made me conclude I'd wasted my time. I shelved the book (so to speak) and told her I'd decided to give up on it. I did ask for the CD back, explaining I had no copy of my own, but somehow that never happened. I dropped the matter. It wasn't worth making her even angrier to keep nagging about an old dream.

***

Mrs. Bale told me on the ride home from Petoskey that her tests had come out okay. After I dropped off at her home, I settled in my own living room with a handful of almonds, a bowl of tomato soup, and a piece of banana bread to watch the evening news. The words "Bay View" caught my ear, and I tuned in. The segment told of an elderly man from Detroit who'd become senile, been institutionalized for years, and finally died. His will revealed he'd had an African wood sculpture he owned hollowed out and made into a safe. Inside it he'd hidden his dead wife's diamond necklace. As far as the heirs could recall, the statue had been last seen at their summer home in Bay View, but there was no sign of it now. The son's wife disliked the primitive piece, and at first he'd accused her of giving it to the Salvation Army. When the woman swore she'd never touched the thing, they realized it must have been stolen.

I immediately thought of my detective story and the events it was based on. Sure enough, the reporter said the couple's house was one that had been robbed a few years back. The son hadn't remembered the African statue until his father's will was read. Now he was offering a reward for its return.

Chapter Seven

Most times when Rachel called, I had a Sarah Leigh story to tell, something she'd done to make me angry or resentful or even amused. I excused my complaining as the need to vent, but I honestly did recognize it as whining. Rachel is my biggest fan and my harshest critic, a paradox that will make sense to any woman with a daughter over thirteen years of age. She was the only one who truly understood the hurt and frustration involved in the female-to-female rivalry I now faced so unwillingly.

My lovely, lively daughter works for a chemical laboratory, doing something only a few science nerd types understand. Rachel usually tells people she's working on a cure for the common cold, because that's easier than explaining her real job.

Not at all a science nerd type, Rachel has my oval face with Ben's coloring, honey-blonde hair and fair skin that turns golden in summer. Her eyes are round and truly green, where mine never decided on a color and settled for hazel. While I fight middle-aged thickening, Rachel at almost thirty is slim and as graceful as a dancer. In addition to all that, my daughter has a way about her those in her field often lack.

People walk away from her feeling good about themselves. I don't know how she does it.

Now that I've listed the positives, I'll admit she has a downside: Rachel is painfully direct. If you ask for an opinion, you get no sugar coating from my girl.

Our weekly calls are lengthy. We like to talk things over and bounce ideas off each other, giving feedback, advice, and encouragement. It's great having someone to discuss things with, even if we repeat ourselves a lot and seldom solve anything.

One day early on in the Sarah Trials, when I'd been stung by her refusal to look directly at me during a meeting we'd attended, Rachel remarked, "I love you, Mom, but your admiration of Sarah Leigh has never made sense to me. You tell what a saint she is, and a lot of people agree, but I always found her a little odd."

It had been suggested before, usually by strangers and always obliquely. From habit I came to my friend's rescue. "She hasn't had it easy."

"Look, I admit she's serene and dedicated to doing good, kind of like I picture Mother Teresa. But there's a side to saints people don't like to recognize. They're so sure of what's right that they see no gray in the world. It makes them hard for us mortals to deal with."

"Rachel!" I was shocked she could question goodness like that, though her words struck a chord I didn't want to consider.

"In the first place, she takes everything that scummy husband of hers says at face value."

"Marv's different, but he's not that bad."

"Yeah, right." She huffed a sigh before continuing. "James Leigh is two years older, but he ended up in my class when he was held back the second time. While I can't say we were friends, we did get thrown together a lot, and I probably knew him as well as anyone at school did."

I recalled that Rachel had been James' defender at times, like in junior high science class when she took him as her lab partner because no one else wanted him. James had probably seen her as a friend, given her tolerance of his surliness and the fact their mothers spent so much time together.

"James would have been labeled emotionally impaired if he'd been tested," Rachel was saying, "but Sarah wouldn't have that. She insisted he'd be fine if she worked with him."

"I remember. She bought books and all sorts of accessories: manipulatives, counting blocks, flash-cards."

"On the surface it seemed like good parenting, but Sarah made James sit at the kitchen table and go over and over his homework until he hated every second of it. If he refused, he got speeches about duty and diligence that made him feel ungrateful, like she was trying and he wasn't."

"Did he try?"

"I think he really did at first, but he has some pretty severe learning disabilities, and they couldn't be fixed just by repeating stuff over and over. James needed professional help."

"Yes, I remember that all that effort didn't change much."

"Around ninth grade, James started doing as little as possible, as if to show his mother she couldn't push him around anymore. I think he felt like he'd disappointed her, and it made all his problems worse."

I resisted this new picture of Sarah, telling myself Rachel didn't understand how responsible a mother feels for her child's education. It wasn't Sarah's fault James was a rebel. "Okay, so James is a mess. That's got nothing to do with Sarah and me."

"I just want you to get that she isn't perfect," Rachel insisted. "When she gets on one of her missions where she thinks she's doing the right thing, she's likely to bulldoze anyone in her way."

"Sarah isn't trying to bulldoze me, Rache. She's trying really hard to pretend I don't exist."

"I'm saying she's got some kind of agenda, Mom, and even good people can do the wrong thing when they're blindly certain they're right."

I wasn't convinced, but I promised myself I'd consider Rachel's argument. If something Sarah found important had clashed with our friendship, it might be causing her to act differently toward me.

It was time for a change of subject. Knowing Rachel enjoyed hearing the Barr twins' adventures, I filled her in on Tom's most recent injury.

"If those kids live to adulthood, they've got a great future in canyon-jumping," Rachel said after hearing the story.

That reminded me of Angie's description of the Red Man cabin, and I related that one. I should mention that Rachel is very patient with my news from home that she probably has no interest in. I ended with, "I remember seeing the place or one very like it."

Rachel surprised me with a memory. "I think it's north of town, on one of those swampy lakes. It always looks the same, like no one's been there for years, and I remember something odd on the front side, like a patch."

While Rachel had never been excited about canoeing with her father and me, she'd done plenty of exploring with her friends during high school. I'm pretty sure kegs were involved, but she was either very moderate or very careful not to be caught.

"If the paper mill owns the land, the cabin's probably rotting away, like Angie said. They have no use for it."

Rachel's thought was similar to mine. "With some repairs, it might be a nice weekend getaway."

"If you ever stopped working long enough to come north for a weekend getaway."

Rachel laughed. "Mom, you sound just like a mom. I'll get up to see you soon, I promise."

"That would be great, Sweetie. You need some time off."

"And," she said to wrap up our conversation, "you need to do something about your ex-friend Sarah, or she's going to drive you nuts."

What I did was give up. I knew Sarah well enough to see she didn't want to solve our problem. She wanted me to disappear from her life, but that wasn't going to happen, given the size of Abaletta and the lives we led. After months of hoping Sarah's animosity would go away, I did the only thing I could. I quietly set about finding places to go where she was not, people to spend time with who didn't spend their time with her. I gave up the lunch-bunch, saying I had too much to do on Saturdays. The other girls made a fuss. Sarah said not a word.

Chapter Eight

Here's how I discovered how wrong a friendship can go. In the checkout line at the grocery store (Abaletta is too small for a supermarket), I heard the two women behind me talking.

"It's just amazing," one said. "Who'd have thought, as quiet as she is and with all the chaos going on in her life, she could manage to do something exciting?" I recognized the voice of Janet Cook, who works at the insurance office.

"Yeah, a hairdresser! Hard to believe." That was Elise Sandovitch, a local teacher.

"I hear it will be out soon."

"I'm going to buy a copy and see what it's like."

"Let me read it when you're done, okay?"

"Just think, you have your hair cut by an author who might be famous someday."

"If she's famous she probably won't cut hair anymore, and I'll have to drive over to Westin," Janet groused.

"Excuse me," I interrupted. "I couldn't help but overhear. Did you say someone's having a book published?"

They both stared like I'd just fallen off the produce shelf. "She's your friend," Janet said, like *Duh!*

"Who?"

"Sarah Leigh. She's got a book coming out."

"Book?" I do know what a book is, but I couldn't think of anything else to say. Sarah had written one?

Needless to say, when the book came out I bought it in hardcover, something I never do. Being the only one who knew my "Sarah problems," Rachel teased me a little. "Are you probing her psyche to find the secret of her transformation?"

"I'm curious, that's all." I didn't admit I'd looked around in the bookstore to be sure no one I knew saw me buying it. I have my pride.

That evening I sat down with a bowl of dried cherries and a Pepsi and began to read. The story concerned a small-town real estate agent who discovered a dead body when she went out to look at some property she was listing. The deceased, the owner of a local tavern not noted for its high-class clientele, had recently told his lady barber he'd be coming into lots of money in the near future. That's as far as I got before becoming so angry I could hardly see the words on the page. It was my book, my story! I sat in my tweed recliner for a long time, the book forgotten on my lap as I burned with indignation.

Once speech without spitting was possible, I called Sarah. All my carefully planned wording fled when she answered, and I blurted, "How could you do it, Sarah?"

"Caroline?"

"You stole my book!"

There was a pause, and I pictured her collecting her resources. Sarah's pale face is free from wrinkles. Her hair is still dark and shiny (as mine is, but the credit goes to Miss Clairol) and her figure is slim. She has an air of meekness, but a person who knows what to look for—like her lifelong friend, maybe—will note a tightening in those mild eyes when there's something going on she doesn't like. Her lips might twitch once, but the calm expression she's trained herself to wear soon returns.

I imagined her angry twitch being replaced by blankness before she answered. "Caroline, I don't know what you're talking about."

"You know perfectly well what I'm talking about. The book you published is mine. You never returned it to me, and now you've stolen it!"

"Are you joking?" Her voice was calm, even cold.

"Sarah, you know I wrote that book!" I was close to

shouting.

"Caroline, you may be feeling a bit jealous, but—"

"Jealous! I am not jealous of you. You're—" I broke off as things I hadn't considered became depressingly clear. Sarah knew that I'd told no one else about my book. She had the CD, and she had the hard copy I'd made and given to her for critiquing. I'd had handwritten notes at one time, but they were long gone. (I can't help it; clutter makes me itch for a trash bag.)

Because I had never imagined I'd have to prove who wrote the book, Sarah held every advantage. She'd probably destroyed the original. People who'd been interviewed about the crimes I based the plot on would remember Sarah calling to check details, not me. There was only my word that I'd written the book, and if I made a fuss I'd look like a jealous cat. My anger turned cold.

"How could you do it, Sarah? We were friends."

"Of course, we're friends, Caroline. Believe me, I'm grateful you helped me get the book started, but you gave up on it, remember? I did the work; I got it published. It's mine. Once you get over this...misunderstanding, you'll realize that and forget this silly accusation. I intend to forget it as soon as I hang up the phone." As I took breath to argue, the icon on my phone indicated the person who'd been on the other end was no longer there.

I spent the next hour making bitter wishes: I wished I had kept a copy of my book, wished I had proof it was my work, and wished—I won't mention all I wished for Sarah Leigh. It's enough to say that by the time a little calm returned, I admitted there was nothing to be done. Sarah had gotten back at me for every slight she placed at my door, real or imagined. My only consolation was that a sequel was highly unlikely.

Move with me to the next day at work. I was still hopping mad at Sarah, and even more so at myself. I entered the break lounge after a particularly trying session with one of our doctors—not one of ours, actually. This one comes periodically from the big hospital, and he feels it's beneath him to have to take his turn at our tiny clinic in tiny Abaletta.

The guy acts like I'm not quite as good a nurse as he's used to or I wouldn't be working in this jerkwater spot. I could have told him I didn't miss working in a mega-hospital with its ever-increasing demands on RNs to do more and more with less and less. At least our people leave feeling like someone noticed them.

Anyway, he was cranky, which didn't help my mood.

When I walked into the lounge and discovered the topic of conversation between my co-workers was Sarah Leigh's new book, I felt sick.

"Hey, Caroline will know. Did Sarah write that story totally from her imagination, or is it based on something factual, like a 'based on real events' thing?" Debbie asked.

"Oh, writing the book was totally her imagination," I almost snarled.

"I suppose you got to read it first," Lou put in. "Giving her feedback and all."

"As a matter of fact, I did read it first."

"It's pretty good, isn't it? I started it yesterday morning and ended up reading half the night. I had to know who the killer was, though Ed was griping about me having the light on." Debbie's face reflected the mystery reader's dilemma: sleep or solution.

"I thought it was pretty good." I hadn't lied yet.

Then Lou Ann said something I simply couldn't deal with. "It must feel great to create something people can't put down. Don't you wish you could write like Sarah Leigh?"

I freely confess that I lost it. "As a matter of fact," I heard myself say as another part of me gasped in horror, "I have a book deal in the works right now." Ignoring the incredulous faces before me I went on, "Actually, I finished mine before Sarah got hers done, but she got lucky on the production end. Different publishers, you know? I got the slow one."

There was a silence in the lounge as the two women stared at me in amazement. If I could have, I'd have looked at myself the same way. I'd told the biggest lie of my life, maybe the only lie that counted for anything. Now I either had to get a book published or be seen as a pitiful wannabe, so jealous of her friend's success that she dreamed up a whopper to make herself look important.

I shut off the chorus of questions from my co-workers, claiming I was legally bound to keep quiet about my work. Then I went to the storage closet, where I succumbed to the reaction to my own stupidity. True, there was a book floating around in my head, but I hadn't put one word on paper yet. Not only did I have to write the thing (and rewrite and rewrite, which I knew from the first one), but I had to find a publisher for it, or I'd never be able to face the world again.

I asked myself, with an accompanying smack to the forehead, how could I have said such a thing? It took me twice as long that day to straighten the supply closet, but it might have been the tears that held me up.

Chapter Nine

So there I was, caught up in a falsehood I knew would spread like wildfire. The idea that one person in Abaletta could get a book published was exciting enough, but when my co-workers announced my book deal to the town—

I was a wreck. I don't know what most people do in these moments, but I called my daughter. Rachel would understand, though first I'd get an earful about my dumb stunt.

Tears threatened at the sound of her voice, but I kept myself in check. When I cry I'm pretty much incoherent, and over the phone that's the worst. "Rachel, you know how upset I've been about Sarah's behavior—"

She started right in. "Mom, I keep telling you to stop obsessing over that woman. She's all duty and no fun, and you're better off without her for a friend."

"It isn't about Sarah and me not getting along anymore." In a few words I told her about the book I'd written. As she often does, my daughter surprised me.

"I knew you had a secret! After Dad died you were down for so long, but then you perked up a little, and you were always at the computer. Once during a visit I tried to get a peek, but I couldn't find the file."

"Rachel Catherine!" I admonished before adding ruefully, "I wish you had seen it, so you could be my witness." I told her about Sarah's newly-published book and my lack of proof it was mine.

"She stole your manuscript?" I imagined Rachel shaking her head. "I knew she wasn't all sweetness and light, but—"

"It gets worse. It made me so mad that I announced I'll have a book published soon."

"You what?"

"I know, it was wrong."

"Wrong? It was just plain dumb, Mom. Do you even have another manuscript?"

"No, but I have an idea."

"An idea." She made it sound like I planned to rewrite *Hamlet* in Sanskrit.

"Listen, Rachel. I did it before. I mean, I don't think Sarah changed my story much."

"I can believe that, if she writes like she styles hair." The joke in town is that everyone who sits down in Sarah's salon chair gets up looking the same. "Friend or enemy, the woman has no creativity in her soul."

"I could write down my new idea for a story. It's a medical murder mystery, based on what I know. Isn't that what they tell you to write about?"

"Yeah, but do they also tell you to write fast, find an agent who'll do miracles, and get your book published in record time so you don't have to admit you lied about it?"

"I really made a mess," I moaned.

As soon as I admit I've screwed up, when I'm about to succumb to hopelessness, my daughter turns cheerleader. "Mom, I'm not saying you can't publish, but it won't be easy."

"I know."

"We'll have to get going right away." Her use of *we* made me feel better immediately. I wasn't alone in this anymore.

"What can I do?"

"Write, write, write, and hope this idea of yours is good. Believe it or not, a guy at the lab who has published a couple of thrillers keeps asking me out. It might be worth dinner if I can get him to approach his agent and recommend you. He says half the battle is getting their attention, because a lot of them only take referrals from people they know."

"Just dinner?" I asked.

"What was that?"

"I said you're only going to have dinner with him. I wouldn't want to be responsible for...anything else."

"Mom, you are *such* a mom!" my daughter chided with a laugh. "I won't sell my body for you. Gerry will gladly talk about himself all evening and go home in a cab."

So the evening of the Day of the Big Lie, after the phone conversation with Rachel, I began writing my second book.

The story I had in mind was, like the earlier one, inspired by real events. A news item had started me thinking again, and I made up a scenario that fit what I knew, filling in with fictional details. I tried not to think about all the hurdles ahead of me on the way to publication.

For the next week I was at my computer whenever I wasn't sleeping or working, and the story took shape nicely. I'd learned a lot from writing the first one, and I kept careful notes. Fifty pages later, it's hard to remember the name of the doctor who pronounced the victim dead at the scene, but you might need him back in the story.

Research is also important, and I gathered every book I thought I might need. I didn't have far to reach for a regular dictionary, a medical dictionary, a thesaurus, and a map of northern Michigan. It's always surprising what I don't know when things get specific: does M33 run all the way to

Mackinaw, or does it end in Cheboygan? Does *defibrillator* have one *l* or two? And the age-old question, what's another word for *said*?

Of course I had to face the speculative glances of neighbors and acquaintances. Most people think that if an author writes a book that's good, it will be published. Unfortunately, there are lots of good writers at any moment in time who are working for their own enjoyment, whether they meant to or not. It was disturbing to imagine future comments if my book never got published. "Guess she just *thought* she was a writer," I could imagine the good people of Abaletta saying. "Now, Sarah Leigh: who knew?"

The local paper had gone wild at the news of Sarah's success, having for once something to write about that people were actually interested in. Sarah Leigh became the focus of a whole edition, aside from the sports news, court news, and a column by a long-retired editor who reports weekly what birds he's seen in his backyard. Otherwise, every article, feature, and letter to the editor concerned our native author.

Sarah was asked her opinion on everything from punctuation to Shakespeare to who should run for President on the Republican ticket. Her life was recorded in some detail, as if everyone reading the paper didn't already know it. In fact, we knew more, because the articles said nothing about James, mentioning only a darling granddaughter the "authoress" claimed was her inspiration and the joy of her life. It interested me to read that the state police had contacted Sarah, wondering if she could shed light on some old, unsolved crimes similar to the ones described in her book. Since in the story the murdered man had hinted to a hairdresser about his involvement in some recent burglaries, they thought she might know something they didn't.

"Your book came from the robberies back then?" Rachel asked me. We spoke daily now, and she was really getting into the saga of Sarah.

"Yes, the basic outline." I was dusting as we talked. I can't get motivated for the job when it's just dusting, but to get it done while talking on the phone somehow provides a double sense of accomplishment. "I thought about how tempting those summer places must be when the owners aren't there."

"Which is most of the time."

"Right. The real thefts seemed targeted, the reports said. Only certain types of things, antiques and curiosities, were taken, and they never resurfaced."

"Sold to private collectors." Rachel reads Clive Cussler, so she knows all about art thieves and their methods.

"The stories of the burglaries interested me, since I've always loved Bay View. Then there was this death that could have been a hunting accident, except it was out of season."

"Oh, come on," Rachel chided, "the locals think any time they're hungry for venison is hunting season."

"I know. But no one knew why this victim was so far from home or why he went walking in the woods in street shoes. The shot was taken at close range too. If it was a violator, he was extremely careless."

"Lots of that kind around too."

"True," I agreed. People often get killed in hunting accidents that would never happen if somebody had an iota of common sense. But since this guy had no reason to be out in the boonies, I thought it made a great mystery scenario."

"They never found who did it?"

"No. Those two stories gave me the idea for my plotline. I made the bar owner-slash-shooting victim part of the burglary ring. He was their wheel man."

Rachel chuckled. "You've got the terminology down."

"It's all those action movies your dad used to make me watch," I joked. A momentary pang of longing for the past hit unexpectedly, as it is wont to do. Long evenings with Ben in front of the TV now seemed the height of happiness. I said nothing about that, unwilling to burden Rachel further with long-distance worry. Instead I redoubled my efforts with the dust rag.

"In my story, the murder victim had hinted to a woman who cut his hair that he was about to make a lucrative deal. That's how my detective linked his death to the art thefts."

"How did your character decide to get a haircut sixty miles from his home town?"

"I gave him a flat tire while he was transporting the stolen goods. While he waits for it to be fixed, he notices the salon and thinks, 'Since I've got to sit around this jerkwater place anyway, might as well accomplish something.'"

"Possible."

"My bad guy knows he's said too much, but he consoles himself with the knowledge this hick-town hairdresser doesn't even know his last name. The cops track him down through the computer at the garage where his tire was fixed."

"Very neat, Mrs. Sherlock."

"Thank you. I like my clues to add up so the reader has a fair shot at the solution."

"But Sarah Leigh can't help the police with the real

murder, since the hairdresser thing never really happened."

"Right. But the novel must have made the real police wonder if the victim and the hairdresser really met."

"I ordered the book," Rachel said. "I can't wait to read it, though I resent that woman profiting from my purchase."

At the bitter tone in Rachel's voice, my automatic defenses kicked in. "Sarah's a good person at heart, Rache."

"Maybe," she replied. "But think *Gone with the Wind*."

I was confused. "The movie?"

"Well, you gave me the book for Christmas when I was sixteen, and I like it better. Either way, Melanie is good and kind and sweeter than molasses, right?"

"Yes."

"Notice she is not the heroine. Everyone loves and respects her, but she isn't the fun one. It's Scarlett we want to know about, Scarlett who makes the book worthwhile."

"Because she's bad."

"Because she's alive, Mom—not so blindly harnessed to propriety she can't enjoy life. Sarah's always been Melanie, respectable and boring. Maybe she's sick of it."

"Does that make me rotten old Scarlett?"

Rachel chuckled. "I don't see you as a spunky Southern belle, just a Michigan hillbilly, feudin' with Sarah Leigh."

"Well," I groused, tossing the dust cloth into the laundry hamper, "I hope she's as embarrassed as heck when the police come to question her."

It wouldn't have come as a surprise to Sarah that my story was based in fact, but the interest of investigators several years afterward must have. Their determination to find a killer was admirable, but no doubt it made "the authoress" nervous to have to speak to the police. She had a lot to hide.

Chapter Ten

Inevitably I ran into Sarah, and unluckily, it was at a very public place: the elementary school. I arrived there a shade after eleven, hurrying because I was late. I'd promised to man the popcorn machine for Treat Day, and I'd almost forgotten, being focused on my writing. By chance I'd had to check a date to make the plot work and saw my note from weeks before: POPCORN.

When I arrived at the alcove where volunteers serve their time, my counterpart was already there, bent over a fifty-pound bag of kernels. "Sorry to be late," I huffed, stripping off the sweater I'd needed two minutes earlier. Tossing it on the seat of a nearby chair, I surveyed the preparations. The aroma of hot oil told me my partner was already heating the kettle, and when she turned, I faced Sarah Leigh. "Oh. Hi." It was all I could manage.

"Hello, Caroline." Sarah had already removed her white cotton over-shirt and hung it neatly on the back of the chair to keep it from wrinkling. "I've started the first batch. While it pops, you might go to the kitchen and see if they've got more salt. We're just about out."

Coward that I am, I went meekly off to find salt.

It seemed Sarah meant to stand by her statement she would forget our phone conversation. Communication for the first hour was limited to: "Could I have some of those bags, please?" and "Certainly."

Inwardly I called myself names for letting her ignore what she'd done. How, though, does a civilized human being deal with another's outright refusal to admit guilt, especially while surrounded by eager children bumping each other around to get to their bags of popcorn?

As we worked, I toyed with the idea of hiring a lawyer, but what then? Would we hold a writing contest? My mind conjured up ridiculous images, like the truth tests of medieval times where Might proved Right. Could I whip Sarah Leigh in a wrestling match? If we walked on hot coals, would her feet blister and mine remain unscathed? I imagined her abject apology once the test was over, but in the end, possession of the manuscript made Sarah its owner. Nothing I said would change that, tests of truth being out of favor in the new millennium.

We worked through lunch period, setting out the last bags of popcorn at twelve-thirty for the fourth graders, who are my favorites. They're old enough to have a miniature sense of maturity but still childish enough to find genuine delight in treats and the ladies who hand them out.

Sarah cleaned the popcorn machine while I swept stray kernels into a dustpan. Despite everything we functioned well together, sharing a dislike of sloppiness. I was feeling almost forgiving when the teacher, Maeve Carson, gushed in a breathy voice, "Children, these two ladies are writers, and someday, when you're older and read really well, you'll be able to buy books by Mrs. Batzer and Mrs. Leigh."

The kids were pretty much unimpressed. One pig-tailed little girl managed a weak, "Wow," as she stepped up to get her popcorn. They trooped off to line up in order outside their classroom door. Maeve is a nosy snoop, but her students know how to behave.

At my side, Sarah had frozen as Maeve's remark penetrated. Was it possible she hadn't yet heard about my book? With a jealous stab, I told myself she was so caught up in her own success she hadn't noticed the little people around her, struggling on in obscurity. Her usual control over her expression failed her as Sarah turned to me with an angry glare. After Maeve moved away she asked coldly, "You're writing a book?"

"A second book actually," I answered just as icily.

Sarah's face paled to the hue of the limestone Abaletta is

known for. "Is there anything of mine you won't try to outdo?" she said through clenched teeth.

It was so unfair. *She* stole *my* work, and now she was accusing me of trying to steal her thunder!

In contrast to her pale iciness, I felt on my neck the telltale flush that signals I'm about to lose my temper. At those moments, I can no more control my tongue than I can stop the red rising up to my cheeks. "If you had done it, Sarah, I'd be the last person to take credit from you. We both know you didn't write *Murder on a Vacant Property,* and I'm going to prove who the real writer is."

Hearing a gasp behind me, I turned. Too late, I saw that Maeve had come back to get one more bag of popcorn.

Though Maeve's face registered shock, there was a hint of glee in her eyes. I'd had the bad luck to have words with Sarah in front of the biggest gossip in the school, maybe in the whole town. I could hear Maeve's breathy voice in my head: "They were *furious* with each other, and I thought they were such good *friends*!"

Both Sarah and I went silent. Sarah's lips clamped tightly together, and I put a hand over my mouth, wishing the words back inside. Pride should have prevented my making accusations I had no way of proving, but I hadn't lasted an afternoon in Sarah's company before losing control. Now I had to prove I could write a book and somehow convince the world Sarah Leigh hadn't written the one published under her name. Neither task was going to be easy to do but if I didn't, I'd be labeled the most envious, back-stabbing best friend on the planet.

Sarah turned away, her back rigid. Her face was expressionless as she picked up her jacket, purse, tote bag, and car keys. Miserably, I watched Maeve bustle back to her classroom. She had something juicy to report in the teacher's lounge, and I knew she couldn't wait to get there.

I longed to put this whole mess behind me, to find out what had made Sarah steal my book, why she was angry with me, and if we could ever be friends again. When I turned back, however, she was already striding up the hall, head high. Hurrying, I caught up with her in the entryway. "Sarah, can we go somewhere and talk?"

"I don't have time, Caroline." Her voice was flat.

I stepped directly in Sarah's path, forcing her to either stop or walk around me. "I need to drive out to the lake and check the cabin roof. Will you ride out there with me?"

As I spoke, the principal's secretary entered the building with the day's mail. The greeting on her face died when she observed our body language. Glancing at the woman, Sarah replied to my request in a tone that was probably more civil than she wanted to be.

"Caroline, you're upset. When you're calm, we'll talk, but right now, I have to go." With that she walked around me as if I were a dirty tennis shoe someone had dropped in the hallway. The look she gave the secretary was a perfect blend of patient forbearance and genteel embarrassment at the scene I had caused.

I must have looked furious, because I was.

I went home, no longer in the mood to check on the cabin, though the roof had begun leaking and I did need to see to it. I told myself I should get some writing time in, but noticing the smell of popcorn on my clothes I changed, gathered a small load, and threw it in the washer. One casualty of widowhood has been weekly laundry. I wash items as I need them and sometimes go for weeks without ever approaching the machine.

After that I wandered the house aimlessly, trying to force myself to get to work. My good intentions degenerated to zero productivity, and I didn't even turn the computer on. What would it accomplish? Who did I think I was, planning publication of a book that wasn't even written yet?

I lay down on the couch, letting my mind replay the scene at the school and trying out ways I might have handled things differently. I hadn't come out well, but Sarah's anger at me had been terrible, worse than all the times I'd imagined a confrontation.

Now everyone would know about the rift between us. They'd speculate on what I'd done to make meek, mild Sarah Leigh reject me. Disgusted, I turned on the TV, found a channel with old *Law & Order* reruns, and alternated between dozing and regretting.

When the doorbell rang I glanced at the clock. It was almost six. Where had the afternoon gone?

Ben hated curtains. He'd claimed windows are meant to be seen through and shouldn't be blocked with fabric. Consequently I could see out the bay window to the front door where Sheriff Damon Bates stood on my porch.

Bates should have a made-for-TV movie where he stars as himself. He's that good looking. The man's kept himself in shape well into middle age and has a presence that makes many lonely widows (and a few non-widows too, I've heard) get that hungry look. Maybe because of it, Damon is reserved with everyone, more so, it's said, since Mrs. Bates left Abaletta looking for a more cosmopolitan lifestyle. His job is complicated now that he's "available," so Bates goes to great lengths to be professional, even distant, with the female sex.

Checking my couch-mashed hair in the hallway mirror (No, I'm not interested, but who wants to be a mess when a visitor shows up?), I fluffed it a bit and went to the door.

"Sheriff, how are you?"

"I'm fine, Mrs. Batzer. May I come in?"

I had a moment of panic, wondering if the airline had sent him with news of some terrible accident involving my son. Damon read the look. "I need to ask a few questions."

The circus, I thought with relief. Every year I buy tickets through the sheriff's department and donate them to disadvantaged children. Still, our handsome sheriff doesn't make personal pleas for funds. "Come in. Can I get you some coffee?"

"No, thanks." He sat on the couch, which I should have steered him away from. He sank so low that his knees almost hit his chin. The couch needed replacing, but whenever I thought of it, an image of Ben appeared in my mind, stretched out for an afternoon nap with his feet sticking off one end and his face buried in the cushions. When that happened, I couldn't give the crummy thing up.

Taking the lumpy sofa well, Bates got down to business. "Mrs. Batzer, where were you this afternoon?"

I wondered why the police cared about my schedule, but taught from childhood to be a good citizen, I was cooperative. "Until twelve-thirty, I was at the school making popcorn, a PTA thing."

"And since then?"

He wanted an hourly report? "I've been here." Unwilling to admit I'd done nothing all afternoon, I added, "Working."

"Working?" His tone was mild, the question direct.

"On my book. I'm..." Should I say I was working on a new book or polishing up the old one? "...writing."

Lame, Caroline!

"Anyone else around?"

I decided to end the polite preliminaries. "Sheriff, tell me what's going on, and I'll answer any questions you have for me."

Bates' handsome face showed reluctant resignation. "Mrs. Leigh is missing, possibly dead."

"Sarah?" Several emotions shot through me as I took in what he'd said. Possibly dead? "Sarah Leigh?"

"I'm afraid she might have been murdered."

Sarah had once been closer to me than a sister, and the first emotions I experienced were shock and grief. As if the last two years had not happened, I felt the loss of my best friend, my lifelong confidante, the person who'd known me better and longer than anyone living. Tears flowed, the kind that can't be delicately wiped away with a tissue, the kind that are accompanied by sobs. For several minutes I was lost in sadness.

Bates sat uncomfortably on my sagging couch until I regained a measure of control. As rational thought returned, I wondered why the news of Sarah's possible death rated a personal report from the authorities. Looking at Sheriff Bates' solemn face, realization dawned. Sarah Leigh was someone half the town knew by now I was furious with, maybe angry enough to kill. When Bates asked if I would accompany him to his office, I was pretty sure it was an order, not a request.

Sarah's van had been found at Shoepac, a lake a few miles outside Abaletta, with the driver's side door open, the keys in the ignition, and her purse on the front seat. In the back was my red sweater, the one I wear so often it's a sort of badge.

I'm at that stage of life where I'm either shivering with cold or pulling off layers like Gypsy Rose Lee. A cardigan is part of every outfit, and I'm fond of red. As we age, we can either add color or look washed-out. Red is good.

Rachel has lectured me on the subject more than once. "Mother, I've bought you nice sweaters the last three years for Christmas, your birthday, and just because I found one you might like. You're saving them for 'good' and wearing that old ratty red one, aren't you?"

I like that one (or dragging it around, depending on my body temperature at the moment).

Why was it in Sarah's van, and how had both gotten to Shoepac Lake?

The area south of Abaletta is karst country, where interesting land formations called *sinkholes* (or simply *sinks*) are found. Bedrock underlying the area is limestone, which can dissolve in the weak acids found in rain water. This forms large underground caves which sometimes collapse, making holes 80 to 100 feet deep in the land surface. Because their steep sides are so dramatic, some sinks have been made into parks with hiking trails around their outer edges for viewing.

Shoepac is one such area, and the lake itself is a sinkhole that filled with water. Because we were avid canoers, Ben and I had bought a cabin out there and spent many happy hours paddling around its shores. Over the years, the sink/lake occasionally widened as the water dissolved yet more of the surrounding land away, and at one point we had witnessed a cave-in. The ground along one section of the lake simply melted away, and in slow and stately style, several trees, along with huge amounts of sand, dirt, rocks, and vegetation, slid into the lake with hardly a sound.

It was both beautiful and awesome to watch as the water, like a terrible fish, swallowed what it was given. The line between shore and lake became an abrupt drop-off. A step on the shore was firm. A step into the water plunged the wader in over his head. It was one of those moments when a person is made to realize how little we matter to the earth.

Considering the depth of Shoepac Lake and the debris lying or leaning in various configurations far below the surface, it's a difficult place to search. With luck, a missing body would surface in time, but if it snagged on a tree branch or got wedged beneath an underwater shelf, it might remain in the lake's depths forever.

Chapter Eleven

It didn't look good when Sheriff Bates laid out the evidence concerning Sarah Leigh's disappearance. She'd left the school in my company, we'd been arguing, and I'd asked her to ride along to the lake. My red sweater in the back seat of Sarah's van was damning, since I'm seldom without it. I could only guess I'd left it behind in my haste. Had Sarah picked it up to return it to me?

No, she'd left first. I'd followed her up the hall.

"From the looks of it," Bates told me, "someone was knocked unconscious with a rock, maybe killed. The victim was tied to something heavy, probably a spare tire, which dragged through the sand behind the body. It was maneuvered into the canoe you keep at your cabin, taken out into the lake, and dropped in. The canoe was returned to shore, and someone headed into the woods, where the trail disappears."

"How terrible!"

Bates rubbed his forehead. "We might not have known about it for days except that some downstate fishermen were scouting lakes in the area. Not normally a lot of traffic out there this time of year."

"It wasn't me, Sheriff. I would never hurt Sarah."

He cleared his throat. "There'd be signs on the person's clothes. Tire dirt, grit from the canoe—maybe blood."

It became hard to breathe. I'd thrown my clothes in the washer because they smelled of popcorn oil. Would Bates think I'd been trying to hide my afternoon's activities?

I was sick at the thought of Sarah's possible death, even more sick that I had no way to prove I hadn't gone with her to Shoepac Lake.

The sheriff seemed confused by my spontaneous emotional outburst. He'd probably expected a tearful confession of temporary insanity, not an outpouring of grief at the loss. Some people might forget the good years because of a couple of bad ones. I could not. Whatever she had done to me, I would miss Sarah Leigh. In fact, I'd missed her for the last two years. If she was gone forever, we could never reconcile. I'd never know what made her turn against me or understand what made her steal my book and publish it under her own name. My friend was gone from me in a dozen different ways, and given the evidence, possibly in the most final way of all.

My reaction, natural and unplanned as it was, couldn't have been more advantageous to my cause. The taciturn

Damon Bates became my defender in those unguarded moments, though he gave no indication at the time.

At the sheriff's office Bates moved into the background, taking no active part in my questioning. An investigator from the state police handled that, a hard-looking man who regarded me as if I might start foaming at the mouth any second.

Sergeant Dean had salt-and-pepper hair that wanted to curl, so it was cropped short. He brought Dudley Do-Right to mind: square chin, high forehead, nose distinctly perpendicular to his cheekbones, but he walked like his knees hurt. His manner indicated a by-the-book type who'd taken in the facts of the case and reached a conclusion that satisfied him.

There had been bad blood between Sarah and me, now she was missing. I had been with her today: motive and opportunity were a given. Since the means was ostensibly a rock and my canoe, I was suspect there too. The working theory was that I'd snapped due to jealousy, killed Sarah, and calmly gone home to do laundry and obliterate the evidence of my crime.

Dean sat in Bates' wooden swivel chair, lined by one of those beaded-wood mats that massage your back while you work. I got a characterless plastic seat whose selling point must have been the fact it could be hosed off in the event of drips, spills, and bodily malfunction. Bates leaned against his file cabinet, ready to fetch whatever the stern-faced state cop might need. I thought it was unfair that he was relegated to bystander, but I supposed he understood the pecking order in such situations better than I.

"Mrs. Batzer, let's begin with your relationship with Sarah Leigh," Dean began. "Things had gotten tense between you, and I'd like to understand why."

I sat back in the chair, hoping he was willing to be patient. "She'd probably tell it differently, but Sarah's been acting weird toward me for some time."

Something in Dean's face warned me to be careful. The sheriff had told me a lawyer could be present during my questioning, but I just wanted to tell them the truth. Dean claimed they were simply gathering information before choosing a direction: dragging the lake or waiting to see if Sarah showed up somewhere. After a few minutes I sensed he'd made up his mind, but I was pretty sure Bates had not.

"People disappear for all sorts of reasons," he'd explained on the drive to his office. "Lots of times they show up again when they're ready." Thinking back on the comment now, I wondered if Bates was suspicious of the scenario at the lake.

Still, the scene indicated foul play, and I was supposed to explain why I wasn't the one responsible. Dean sat expectantly as I fumbled for a place to begin. Would it make sense to someone unaware of how extreme Sarah's change of attitude toward me had been? How far back should the explanation start?

I stuck to the facts, avoiding any attempt to explain emotional facets. Sarah for some unknown reason had stolen a book I wrote and claimed it as her own. Yes, I had confronted her about it, but I was working on my own writing career and was willing to let published works speak for my authorship. I'd been at home all afternoon.

"Did you invite Mrs. Leigh to go to Shoepac Lake with you today?" Dean asked.

"I wanted us to talk things through, but she refused."

"And you didn't go there?"

"You can tell my car hasn't been out there. This time of year it would be a mess if it had."

"But if you rode out there with Mrs. Leigh—"

"I'd have had to walk more than ten miles back home."

Dean didn't like that part, but he didn't argue.

At that moment a deputy from the front desk knocked deferentially and said, "Call for you, Sergeant."

With a nod to Bates, Dean took the call. We sat silent as he went through some preliminaries, explaining to someone the details of Sarah's disappearance. As he listened, frown lines appeared on his forehead and deepened to a scowl. "I see. Well, there's a development here you should know about then. It seems someone else might have written the book." As Dean went on telling my story to some unknown, I sat listening in confusion. What had all this to do with Sarah's—my—novel?

The upshot of the call was that I had to wait in Bates' office while a second state police officer drove up from a different state police post. This one, Detective Homer Oskar, had recently spoken to Sarah by phone.

As we waited, Dean went over the events of the day several times, trying to find a hole in my story. I answered his questions honestly but with no embellishment. His manner grew frustrated when he failed to get me to admit to leaving home all afternoon. It was clear he considered no suspects but me, no scenario other than the obvious one.

Chapter Twelve

When Detective Oskar arrived he took over, but nobody seemed resentful. Bates and Dean retired to a local restaurant for dinner, and I was left with the detective and the promise of take-out chicken wings when Bates returned.

Oskar was a lot like Dean in appearance: smoothly groomed and shaven, tall and fit. They differed in manner though. I got the impression this man looked carefully at all the evidence before drawing conclusions. Hopefully he and Sheriff Bates would counter Dean's rush to judgment.

Before he ever asked a question, Oskar gave me his history with Sarah Leigh. Settling into Bates' creaky old chair he began, "I planned to speak with Mrs. Leigh about an interesting correlation between the book she—" He changed the word he'd intended."—published and some crimes we investigated a couple of years back. I bought the book mostly out of curiosity, since it was by a local author. But as I read, I began seeing similarities to two cases I'm aware of. One was a series of art thefts I worked on personally. The other I only read about. At the time we didn't connect them. Later, following up on some leads on my case, I got a connection to the Bar-None Bar in Ridgely."

"The place the gunshot victim owned," I put in.

"Yes. We never arrested anyone for either crime, but I liked a particular character as a suspect. Ever hear of a child actor named Rusty Rains?"

"Doesn't sound familiar."

"You might recognize him if you saw his picture. He was on a couple of sitcoms back in the '80s, playing the bratty youngest kid."

"I was never much for sitcoms."

Oskar shrugged. "He was pretty good, maybe because he wasn't acting. These days Rusty goes by his real name, Russell Ranett. Hollywood got fed up with his difficulties with booze and the law about twenty years ago. Russ gave up acting, along with most other legal ways of making a living."

"I'm guessing he moved to northern Michigan."

"I'm not sure why, but yeah, we got him." Oskar sipped from the foam cup Damon had provided and raised his eyebrows, evidently pleased at the quality of the coffee.

"Ranett has a genius for avoiding punishment, and in my opinion, he's capable of anything except compassion. He doesn't usually go in for violent crimes, but he also doesn't worry much if someone who gets in his way is hurt. We suspect him of lots of things we've never managed to prove. Russ has done minor time, but if I'm correct, not nearly as much as he deserves."

"And he connects to the Bar-None?"

"Yes. A witness, an old girlfriend of his, claimed they drove over there several times. Russ always went inside alone, and that isn't like him. The guy likes to make an entrance, and the girl is a looker, whatever else she lacks. I asked myself, 'Why would he leave her sitting in the car?'"

"So when the owner of the Bar-None turned up dead, you thought of this Ranett? Russ?"

"Not till lately. As I said, I was working on the art thefts, and Marilyn—that's the girlfriend—was one of many people we interviewed. I looked at Ranett mostly because of his past behavior, since there was nothing concrete to tie him to the thefts. Marilyn's mention of the trips to the bar was more whining than anything else. She was bored waiting in the car and wondered if he had something going with the barmaid." He chuckled. "Marilyn is not what you would call secure in her self-image."

I smiled at his ironic understatement, but in my head I was matching what I knew of the case with the new information. "You wonder if he was meeting an accomplice."

"I've done some checking. Pete Miltowski, former owner of the Bar-None, had a juvenile record a mile long: vandalism, unlawful entry, things like that. He spent some time in the system and eventually went into the military. Pretty common for the type, somebody figures the army will straighten the kid out."

"It happens."

"It seemed to with Pete. He did a couple tours then left the service. The guy who sold him the bar was looking to retire to Florida, so there was nothing suspicious in the transaction. Pete's sister is a real estate agent, Angela...Something. She helped him set up the deal." He consulted his notes with a frown. "Angela Barr, that's it."

"I've met her," I said. "She mentioned her brother Pete came to a bad end, but I didn't make the connection." I told Oskar about the twins and their frequent hospital visits.

"Interesting." He made a brief notation. "Anyway, Pete ran the Bar-None. Most of his customers aren't candidates for the good citizen award, but he did a decent amount of business."

Oskar's tone hinted there was more to it and I said, "You think Pete wanted more out of life."

The detective smiled. "That's my theory."

People think owning a small business in God's country will be heaven, but they often discover it isn't. A small business can be a millstone, requiring the owner's daily presence to turn even a small profit. Crimes like arson sometimes crop up, or less than honest owners augment their income with illegal sidelines like selling drugs or stolen goods. Pete's disappointment in his bar business might well have brought a return to his youthful lawlessness.

Stretching his long legs out at the side of Damon's desk, the first sign of relaxation he'd shown in my presence, Oskar summed up his findings. He'd decided to trust me, at least a little.

"One thing Pete was into was what he called antiques. Mostly it was second-hand stuff, but he went to auctions, met people in the business, and picked up contacts and information. I figure he might be the link, the guy with the connections to sell items stolen from the homes in Bay View."

"He'd know which dealers wouldn't ask questions if they could get their hands on something unique."

Oskar nodded. "I picture it like this: Russ meets Pete, probably at the bar, but who knows? People of that element tend to gravitate toward each other." Oskar sounded like he'd met a few too many of the type to be empathetic. "They recognize each other as kindred spirits, dreaming of an easy life from a quick score. Russ lives in Petoskey, and let's say he's got an in with someone who comes and goes freely from those fancy homes. Not knowing who that is bothers me, because he or she is probably still there."

"Nobody's left the area in three years?"

"Sure they have, but I've kept track as best I can, and it's all predictable. Kids who worked as cleaners or landscapers go back to college. Women who were caterers or nannies move to other jobs or retire. Nothing that strikes me as odd." He paused, remembering. "There was a guy who used to wander Bay View all winter, and we looked at him pretty close, but he died and nothing came of it."

"Natural causes?"

"I guess so, if drowning is natural. He was definitely an odd duck. Considered himself an auxiliary security guard for Bay View because his family owned a home there back in the 1800s. The real security guys let him have his little delusion, because he was harmless. All winter long he'd snowshoe through the streets every week or so and then report to the association office that all was well."

"A local with a Batman complex?"

"Yeah. His name was Joe Freiburger, but everyone called

him Old Joe. He insisted he'd have seen people hanging around those houses, but obviously he didn't."

"Could he have been in on it?"

"Joe wasn't the type to care about money—or if he did, he didn't spend it on things like electricity. He lived in this run-down little house in Petoskey that was so dark I could hardly see my hand in front of my face. No TV, not much furniture, either. I guess those big houses seemed like palaces to him, so he made it his personal mission to protect them."

I pictured the community I'd recently driven through with Mrs. Bale: the steep hillside rising along Little Traverse Bay and all those grand Victorian manors. It wasn't that surprising that a man living in squalor, a guy with no other purpose in life, might consider it his mission to guard them.

"You'd think a man his age would know better than to fish thin ice, but they say Old Joe drank a bit."

Another fudgie-type mistake. Seasoned fishermen watch closely for changes in temperature and wind direction so they don't end up under the ice or trapped on a floating chunk in the middle of Lake Michigan. A man who'd lived up north all his life should have been better able to judge the ice's thickness and character.

Oskar came back to his point. "Anyway, it was another

blind alley. Nothing we found in Joe's house connected him to the robberies. Nobody else we looked at came into large sums of money and started living high on the hog. Nothing screamed, 'This isn't right.'"

"So you were at a standstill."

"Until this book came out." Damon Bates stood in the doorway, his gray eyes directed at me. Behind him Dean peered around him as if trying to see if I was in handcuffs yet.

Oskar nodded at them, and they entered and sat in the two remaining chairs. I smelled fry grease as Bates set a takeout carton on the desk before me. I'd thought I was hungry, but my stomach didn't respond well. I thanked him but left the meal where it sat.

"Right. The book linked the burglaries to the supposed hunting accident," Oskar said. "When I read that, things started clicking in my head. The girl's claim Russ had visited the Bar-None and left her in the car. Miltowski's record of juvenile theft and his sideline as a second-hand dealer. The fact that he wasn't wearing a winter coat when they found him, like he'd gone in someone's car, intending to be right back. Bushwhacking a partner is exactly the kind of thing I'd expect from Ranett."

He closed his notebook with a snap. "The problem is that

Russ still lives in the same crummy apartment, still goes to his job at some little factory every day. If the guy had money, he wouldn't be working for a living, I promise you."

"The story was pure fantasy on my part," I told him. "I read the news stories and made up my own version."

"I got a call about the case back when it was active. Was that you?"

I grimaced. "Sarah, the woman who's missing, was excited about my attempt to write and thought details would make the story more realistic. For instance, we wondered why there weren't alarms."

Oskar clicked his tongue. "You'd be surprised at how many people assume things are safer up here in the north."

"Why do they leave valuable items in their houses?"

"Over the years, things get moved around. People move. They hire professional decorators, who bring in new stuff. Maybe the second wife doesn't like the painting the first wife bought, but it's too valuable to throw away, so they haul it up north. Or Grandma's jewelry, tacky but not cheap, gets stored at the other house. Some of the owners are third or fourth generation. They don't even realize what's shoved into the corners in those musty old places."

I shook my head. "I wouldn't know what that's like."

"Me either." Oskar shifted in the chair. "No inside information, then?"

"Just the inside of my head, I'm afraid. I put the hairdresser bit in because of Sarah."

"And you wrote the book." Oskar regarded me directly, probably wondering whether to believe me or the woman whose name was listed on the cover. "When I called Mrs. Leigh, I sensed she was reluctant to talk to me."

There must have been a great deal of pressure on Sarah. She'd failed to foresee the results of her action, failed to recognize that people would expect things of her she couldn't manage. Her outburst at the school had probably been fueled by fear the world would discover her secret.

"I don't know why Sarah passed the book off as hers, and I don't know where she is now." I found myself getting emotional again. If Sarah was dead, I was in all kinds of trouble. Why was fear for her safety uppermost in my consciousness?

Oskar slapped his hands to his knees in a gesture of finality. "Well, then, I guess I drove down here for nothing."

I was shocked. My assumption had been this guy was

going to solve everything, and here he was, washing his hands of me like Pontius Pilate.

"But Sarah's missing, and they think I killed her!" The protest burst from my lips before I could stop it.

"I'm sure that will be cleared up soon," Oskar said coolly. "Sergeant Dean will keep me informed."

Oskar had had his own reasons for coming. He didn't care who wrote the book or where Sarah Leigh was. He was merely covering all the bases that might lead to his favorite felon's arrest.

The three men left. Damon Bates was the only one who even looked at me. His glance was meant to be encouraging, but I thought I saw worry in the set of his jaw. They went only as far as the room next door, and thanks to thin walls and male voices, their discussion of the situation came through almost as well as if they'd held it in front of me.

Oskar had learned nothing he found of value, but he thanked Damon for his courtesy. Sergeant Dean didn't pull any punches. In his view, I'd done something to Sarah Leigh, and he wanted to arrest me. "She's a widow, and that makes some people squirrely. Could be hormones too. She's at the age when nobody knows what a woman will do."

I quelled a growl of outrage. Dean could make those statements about his own wife—if she'd let him get away with it. Not being prone to hormonal homicide, I resented his generalization.

Damon, who'd let Dean and Oskar have their way thus far, now took a stronger stand. "You don't know Caroline, Sergeant, and I do. You didn't see her reaction when I told her about Mrs. Leigh. She was surprised, and she was sad."

In the end, Bates' arguments left me a free woman, that and the fact I was almost certain to remain in the town where I'd lived my whole life.

Of course I had to face the people I'd known all those years, the good ones and the gossipy ones. The big news was that two state police officers had questioned me, and by morning a large percentage Abaletta's population was convinced that Sarah Leigh was dead, and I was to blame.

Chapter Thirteen

"I can be home by noon," Rachel said when I called. I'd waited to tell her the news until the next morning. No sense in both of us losing sleep.

"Honey, what good will that do? They didn't arrest me, and if they find Sarah or something that exonerates me, I'll be fine. If they do arrest me," I held my voice steady as I said this, "you can be here with a lawyer in no time."

"All right," she agreed reluctantly, "but only because I trust Damon Bates to be fair. He likes you, you know."

"I suppose he does. I don't often commit crimes, so I make his job that much easier."

"I don't mean he likes you, I mean he *likes* you, in the junior high sense."

"Rachel, that's ridiculous." But Diane's comment about a man interested in me came to mind. "Damon Bates?"

"They say he's been asking about you."

"Oh, good grief. You heard this in Chicago?"

"I'm not totally without resources."

"Well, it's just silly. The man is never more than polite,

and he's certainly made no attempt to—to connect." The whole prospect was embarrassing to consider. The fumbling uncertainties of courtship were long behind me, and I hadn't expected to face them ever again.

"Just be cool, Mom. Let him make the first move."

I couldn't help but snicker. "If Damon's first move is arrest, I don't like his odds for getting to second base."

When he came to the house an hour later, I didn't have time to consider our sheriff's motives. I was trying to shed Si Merritt, an elderly client of our clinic who'd heard about my problem and come to assure me of his support. People of his ilk are the best argument in the world against the average citizen having a scanner. There'd been no word about Sarah, I was stressed to the point of screaming, and Si didn't seem inclined to leave me alone, even after he'd said his piece.

A nice old guy with oversized glasses that make his eyes look kind of goofy and a mouth that operates like a mousetrap, snapping shut after each utterance, Si had just repeated for the fifth time his complete faith in my innocence. He was outraged they would even consider arresting someone whose life's work was helping others. He'd just said with a decisive snap that he'd take the matter up with the sheriff when Damon pulled into the driveway.

Si blinked several times, as if he thought he'd somehow conjured Sheriff Bates with a magical repetition of his name. I got nervous, knowing my neighbors would note the return of the police car. Damon slid smoothly out of the vehicle and approached the front door, sensing what was needed.

"Good morning, Mr. Merritt, good to see you." He chatted briefly about the weather then said casually, "If you'll excuse us, I need to speak with Mrs. Batzer, catch her up on what we know."

Damon had accomplished two things at once: he'd gotten the old man to leave and also hinted at his belief in my innocence. I was grateful as the frail Si departed, leaning heavily on his three-footed cane and looking pleased he'd made a stand.

Despite that, the report Damon gave wasn't good. Along with Maeve's witnessing of my accusations, the secretary had reported my request that Sarah go with me to the lake. She'd gone into the office and didn't know if we left together or not. Then of course there was my red sweater, with the little tag sewn inside the neckline: KNITTED FOR CAROLINE BY MOM.

"So Sergeant Dean thinks I talked Sarah into going with me to the lake and then killed her?"

Damon looked embarrassed. "There's something else.

Mrs. Leigh sent a letter to her lawyer, to be opened in the event that anything happened to her. It says you threatened her life because you have some sort of delusion about her and the book she published."

"*I* have delusions? It's Sarah who was having delusions."

Damon tilted his head a little to one side. "Why, Caroline? What happened between you?"

I shook my head. "I don't know. She changed so much a year or so ago that I have no idea what she was thinking."

"I see." He clearly didn't but maintained professional detachment. One of us was crazy, but Damon seemed willing to defer judgment. It was all I could hope for at present.

The hardest part of learning about the letter was it meant Sarah had wanted me to be a suspect. Was it possible she had gone so far as to kill herself to get back at me for whatever she imagined I'd done?

Rachel was furious when I told her about the letter. She insisted I contact a lawyer, and I was willing. "The problem is that the only lawyer I know is Tom Finch."

"Who deals mostly with wills and deeds," Rachel said.

"He's the Leigh's lawyer too, so he'd have a conflict of interest, even if he would take a criminal case."

"I'll see what I can do." Rachel paused, adding, "Mom, this will be cleared up soon."

I couldn't keep my reply from sounding bitter. "I don't see how. I have no alibi, I'm the only person in town with a grudge against the woman, and I asked her to go with me to the lake in front of a witness. How far will they look for another suspect?"

"Maybe it wasn't personal. Maybe some pervert saw Sarah alone out at the lake."

"Why was she there? She said she didn't have time to go with me."

"Maybe she decided you two should talk after all. She went to Shoepac to find you and a crazy person grabbed her."

I couldn't help but smile. "That's my alternative theory? A crazy person hanging out at Shoepac Lake in March?"

"They're everywhere these days." Rachel added firmly, "And if you want my opinion, Sarah Leigh is one of them."

We ended the call, I tried to calm my frayed nerves without her assuring presence in my ear. It did no good to fret over things I couldn't change. I had to figure the situation out before someone at the D.A.'s office overruled Damon Bates and demanded my arrest. There wasn't a lot of time. If they concluded Sarah was indeed the victim of foul play, which seemed likely, I was the primary suspect.

There were things working on my side, and I was glad the sheriff was willing to consider them. My contention I had written Sarah's book opened the possibility that she was not as honest as she seemed. And the note left behind, if not taken at face value, meant she was paranoid at the least, and at most, actively planning to make me look guilty of something.

Neither of us was known as a liar. Of course, I had lied about the second book, a fact that would eventually come out, but Sarah had lied about the first one. That made us even, at least in my mind.

I felt half sick as the day's events swirled in my head. Was Sarah dead or not? If she wasn't, where was she and why had she done this to me? There was nothing in our decades of acquaintance that helped me understand what was going on, and I had no idea what could.

I jumped as the phone at my elbow rang, and I fumbled with the buttons as I answered. "Caroline? It's Bernice." The voice was familiar, and I pictured the lanky brunette at the Cutty Corner, the shop where Sarah worked.

"Hi, Bernice." I was guarded, not knowing what Sarah

had told her co-workers about me.

I needn't have worried. Bernice was as friendly as always. A good-hearted woman who can outwork most men, she has a booming voice and hardly any chest at all. Nevertheless, Bernice is all woman and downright motherly.

"I just want you to know this stuff about Sarah is crazy," she began. "I don't know what's going on, but anyone who says you had anything to do with it is an idiot."

That told me there were people saying things, but I'd guessed that anyway. "Thanks, Bernice. I don't know what to think either." I decided to take advantage of the opportunity offered. "Did she say anything to you about all this? Or has she been acting funny?"

Bernice considered. "Nothing in particular, but I think Sarah's been unhappy for a long time."

"Yes, things haven't always been good for her."

"I don't mean just her idiot husband and her idiot kid, though they're enough to make anyone nuts. Sarah wasn't happy about that book. She didn't want to talk about it, even though everyone else who came into the shop wanted to."

That was understandable in the circumstances. Bernice was still talking, though, and I picked up mid-sentence.

"—is always after her for money, and he brings that little girl in with him every time. James isn't very smart, but he knows Sarah can't say no to that child."

"Yes, Spring's a doll," I murmured.

"Nothing like her dad, or her mom, what I remember of her." Bernice was chewing gum, as usual, and I heard it crack before she spoke again. "I can't stand that James. I try to be polite for Sarah's sake, but he brags constantly, whether he knows what he's talking about or not. Usually not."

"He can be overbearing," I admitted.

"You ask me, I think the little girl's scared of him."

"Scared? Of her dad?"

Bernice backtracked. "I'm not saying I know anything. It just seems like she's nervous when he's around. If it's just her and Nana Leigh, Spring's a whole different kid. You must have seen the difference."

"To tell you the truth, Bernice, I haven't seen much of Sarah lately. After Ben died we grew apart, I guess."

"Yeah, that happens. Though I'd think you'd get closer. You bein' alone and Sarah might as well be."

I don't remember thinking it at the time, but Bernice was right. After Ben died, Sarah and I had been closer than ever, until she changed so drastically. Would I have noticed the signs of her unhappiness earlier if I hadn't been grieving?

After urging me once again not to worry, Bernice hung up. That was easy for her to say. I was grateful, though. It was nice to have someone who knew both Sarah and me affirm her belief in my innocence.

The phone calls continued. Twice it was friends wanting to reassure me things would be okay. One of them was sincere; the other was clearly trolling for details. After that came a call from a reporter asking for a statement on the disappearance of my best friend. I was politely non-committal, but when two more such contacts followed, I began ignoring calls from numbers I didn't recognize.

The last straw was Lloyd Pulanski, a local mail-order-ordained minister who was willing to come over and keep me company "in my hour of need." Lloyd offers his presence and support to widows, old maids, and women whose husbands are away on hunting trips to Canada. In fact, he'll comfort any female who might let him lay his mitts on her. Lloyd always manages to "accidentally" brush my chest when he opens a door or passes me in a crowd. With a shudder, I told him I'd pass then turned off my phone for an hour or so.

I turned it on again around noon, anxious for news from

the police. It didn't ring until Rachel called on her lunch to give me a dose of moral support. I caught her up on the news as I chopped a pepper up for a salad, concluding with, "I need to talk to Marv."

"I thought about that too, but I don't know, Mom. He might not want to talk to either of us." Again her use of the word *us* made me feel a tick better. Love and support from family make a world of difference in a bad situation.

"But Damon can't hold out against the state police forever. In Dean's mind, I did something to Sarah."

"It'll take more than *Damon*'s opinion to get an indictment," Rachel argued, stressing his name to let me know she'd noticed I thought of him more familiarly of late.

I ignored her little joke. "If they don't look any farther than me for a suspect, the details will get fuzzier and fuzzier."

"You aren't equipped to investigate anything." I think she knew I was determined to, equipped or not.

"I think Sheriff Bates will help. He isn't buying the easy answer."

"Of course he isn't. He's known you too long to think you'd kill somebody. Why don't you leave it up to him and the others in town who have a little common sense? They'll convince that state cop it couldn't have been you."

"You're probably right."

But after we ended our call, I still felt that I had to speak to Marv. Sarah was my oldest friend. Now that she was missing, perhaps dead, I wanted to make sure her husband understood that I had had nothing to do with her disappearance.

Chapter Fourteen

Marv Leigh was born to be a used car salesman. He owned a small lot across from the Lutheran church in Abaletta with a bump-and-paint shop in the back where two employees got the cars looking good. Marv was your best friend before he'd known you five minutes, a master at repeating your name with confidence, shining his tilted smile at the right moments, and chucking you fondly on the arm to seal the deal. As far as I knew, the only ones he cheated outright were the insurance companies, and that, he'd tell you, was just business.

Marv was chatty in social situations and always willing to pay his share of the check. His conversation was lively if a little shallow, and he always had a new blond joke, funny and not too off-color. Despite that, Ben never once invited Marv to go hunting with him or to visit the pit when he took his car to the racetrack. Ben was pleasant when thrown together with Marv, but they never got close. If I had to guess why Ben avoided Marv, I'd say his comments about women had something to do with it.

Marv noticed every female in every situation and often pointed out their physical qualities, even in front of his wife.

Back when Ben and I were first married, Marv often commented on my attractiveness, adding each time, "We're lucky to be out with the two most beautiful women in town, Ben." Sarah always blushed when he said things like that. At first I thought it was from pleasure, but as time went on I wasn't so sure. Once as we were talking (when we still were) she told me Marv had suggested she get breast enhancement.

I frowned. "I didn't know you wanted that."

"I don't. At least I never thought I did." She attempted a smile.

"Oh." I was at a loss. So much for Marv's talk about the two most beautiful women in town.

Determined to speak to Marv one-on-one, I drove to the Leigh home. As I pulled in, he opened the door with a hopeful expression that disappeared quickly, replaced by a flat look of animosity. Gossip had done its work.

As I approached, rumors I'd heard about Marv lately returned to the fore. His eyes were red, not the redness of tears but the long-term, rheumy look of blood vessels distended by alcohol. In his hand a can of beer rested naturally, as if seldom absent. I'd heard right then. Marv had taken to drinking more than usual in the past year. He swayed the tiniest bit as he watched me come up the walk.

Leaning a hand against the door frame steadied his stance.

"What do you want?" His dark eyes met mine for once.

I was direct. "Marv, I know you don't believe I had anything to do with Sarah's disappearance."

He tried to maintain his anger, but there was no substance to it. The man had known me all my life, and he couldn't pretend face-to-face that he thought I was the kind of person who'd take his wife to a deserted place and do away with her. His shoulders slumped, and for a minute I thought he'd cry, but he straightened his spine and stepped back, indicating I should enter.

Sarah's house was as tidy as usual except for the area around Marv's chair, a dilapidated recliner in red and yellow plaid that had sat in that spot since I could remember. It was flanked by piles of catalogs: *Northern Outfitters, Cabela's, Gun Enthusiast,* and *Hunter's Review* were the titles I could see. The piles were topped with beer cans, a half-empty chip bag, a dozen cellophane wrappers, and an opened bag of chocolate-covered peanuts. Evidently stress made Marv a compulsive eater.

The rest of the house was Spartan, everything ordered and orderly with no unnecessary additions. The couch was a dull brown, and the walls had only one grouping of pictures for decoration, most of granddaughter Spring. Two fading color photos showed Marv and Sarah in unnatural poses, one commemorating their engagement, the other their wedding. In both of them Sarah appeared to be clinging to a disinterested Marv, her eyes on him while he stared ahead at something of more interest.

There were no plants, doilies, silk flowers, knick-knacks, souvenirs, or mementos. It was almost as if Sarah didn't live in her home but spent her energy elsewhere. Belatedly I realized every good thing in Sarah's life was outside this place, and aside from keeping it spotless, as a good wife does, she invested nothing in it.

I entered the living room, sidestepping Marv's mess, and sat on the couch facing him. "Marv," I began before my courage failed, "Sarah's been angry with me for quite a while, and I don't know why. Now she's disappeared, leaving a letter that says I might be responsible. I would never do anything to hurt her, so why would she say that?"

Marv always looks a little shifty, a too-easy smile and that ingenuous tilt of the head I've come to believe indicates he's about to tell a lie. I saw that tilt now, though the smile was missing. "She never said a word to me about it."

Nursing teaches patience, and I've learned that expectant

waiting often brings a rush of unintentional information. Marv took a sip of beer, glanced at me, and finally broke the silence. "You haven't been together as much lately, but people get busy, and Sarah is sure involved in things."

More waiting. A wheedling tone in Marv's voice communicated tension, and he took a gulping drink from the can. "These fights you women have," he said after swallowing. "Us men can't figure them out."

I frowned slightly as if in anticipation of further revelation. Finally Marv mumbled into his beer can, "Sarah said something once about you always getting everything you wanted dropped in your lap." He finished the beer to hide his discomfort, but when it was gone he stared at the can, studiously avoiding my gaze.

Had Sarah tired of her life? With disappointing kids, no leading roles to play, and no joy in her marriage, had she reached a point where she became angry, even vindictive? If so, I'd become the target of her resentment. What was it she thought I'd done?

Marv knew something, but I wasn't going to get it out of him. He must have guessed I only tolerated him because he was Sarah's husband and she thought the sun rose and set on his command.

I had often tried to see Marv through Sarah's eyes. He was handsome, if you discounted the present signs of too much alcohol and a sleepless night. Handsome but selfish. His free time was spent hunting and drinking—sometimes all night, I'd heard. Sarah accepted every excuse and believed every brag he made about how well he'd done at cards or how much he'd impressed his buddies.

Ben and I had landed on the lucky end of the marriage spectrum, with absolute faith in each other and unquestioned love in every decision either of us made. There were many things about her marriage Sarah must have thought I'd never understand. Suddenly her bitterness against me took on a different aspect. Maybe it wasn't something I'd done. It might have been what I had: my husband's attention and affection.

Sarah had spent thirty years pretending things were okay, and I had let her. Had my childhood friend thought me uncaring when I'd thought I was being diplomatic? Should I have made it my business to encourage her to leave a bad marriage? At times I'd been tempted to give an opinion, but in the end, each person decides what she'll tolerate. Sarah had to know I cared about her. It was unsettling to think I'd become the focus of so much resentment she could no longer abide my presence.

I went over the last few days with Marv, trying to find something in Sarah's behavior to reveal what she'd been thinking. He claimed Sarah had been "funny" toward him for some time. "Spring was the only thing we could talk about anymore," he said resentfully. "If it wasn't about the baby, there was no sense bringing it up."

Marv said he'd gone to work on Wednesday believing things were fine. Late in the day he'd been contacted by the police and had waited for word ever since. He had no light to shed on Sarah's reason for condemning me in her letter, in fact hadn't known she'd written such a document. Still, there was a feral sort of avoidance in his gaze, an unconscious tensing of his shoulders that indicated there was more he could have told me. He was worried about Sarah, but there was something else, something he was ashamed of. When I finally left, Marv was headed to the kitchen to get another beer.

Chapter Fifteen

"There was a lot Marv wasn't saying," I told Rachel that evening on the phone, "but I doubt he killed Sarah."

Rachel snorted sarcastically. "Not likely old Marv would do in the woman who waited on him hand and foot, let him run as he pleased, and settled for an occasional pat on the head like a big old yellow Lab."

I was surprised by the bitterness in Rachel's voice. Though she'd never been fond of Marv, she'd never said so openly before. "Is he really that bad?"

"Mom, didn't Sarah ever confide in you about him?"

"Not really. I know Marv takes advantage of her good nature, but Sarah never criticized him. In fact the way she used to tell it, Marv was every woman's dream man."

"He runs around."

I had trouble at first taking her meaning. Marv was shallow and selfish, but I'd never dreamed he was unfaithful to Sarah. I'd told myself the overnight absences were Marv sleeping off a drunk somewhere. Ben's dislike of Marv's comments about beautiful women finally made sense.

"Your dad never said a word."

"He probably figured it was better if you didn't know. You

never could hide your opinions.”

As I’ve already admitted, I don’t deal well with people I can’t respect. “How do you know so much about Marv’s sins?”

“James told me a long time ago, back when we were teens. It’s gone on almost from day one of the marriage.”

No wonder James had so much anger. “Sarah can’t know about it.”

“Mom.” Rachel’s tone said, *Oh come now.*

“She never let on.” I moaned softly. “All those times I blathered on about Ben. I could slap myself.”

Rachel sighed. “I don’t think people like Sarah share their real selves with anyone. They try to be like everyone else because they think everyone else is doing the same thing.”

“But if you knew Marv slept around, other people must too. How could he treat her that way?”

“Marv is pure sleaze, but in his defense, he was never cut out to marry someone as dull as Sarah.”

I hurried to counter her statement. “She isn’t dull, not really. Sarah’s really smart.” I tried to come up with a way to express Sarah’s quiet wisdom. “It takes her a while to warm up to people, so they don’t get to see how intelligent she is.”

"Mom, she's forty-eight. Isn't it time she started warming up to people she's known all her life?" Rachel's tone was amused. "You know what I think? In your childhood you formed some belief that Sarah is the epitome of goodness, and you can't get past it."

I examined the truth of that. All my life people had pointed out Sarah's virtues. Was it possible that through "Sarah this" and "Sarah that," I had gradually absorbed an unquestioning belief she had no failings? If Rachel was correct, Sarah's strength was also her weakness. Could she have kept her husband's interest and earned her children's affection if she'd been less dogmatic, more approachable?

"Be honest, Mom," Rachel said. "Sarah and Marv were a bad match. In this century that kind of marriage doesn't have to continue for thirty years, but she was too timid to stand up for herself."

"But everyone in town says—"

"That she's a saint. I know. And people like her need that kind of recognition. Where would charities big and small be without the Sarahs of the world to do the dog work?

"My daughter is a cynic!" I exclaimed.

"Sometimes," Rachel agreed. "But Sarah would never have been included in a lot of things if it hadn't been for her association with you. You, Caroline Batzer, pulled her out of that lifeless house and got her involved in the activities she's admired for. You convinced her she could do them, and you were so proud of her you almost split whenever she got any kind of recognition. But remember, you're the Einstein. She's the drone."

"Now my child mixes metaphors." My joke was an attempt to cover my embarrassment.

Rachel chuckled too, but we stopped at the realization we spoke of a possible murder victim. "I wish I knew what Marv isn't telling," I muttered.

"The police will get it out of him eventually." Rachel sighed. "But if he isn't responsible for Sarah's disappearance, whatever he's holding back won't help."

"If all this is Sarah's way of leaving him, I could understand it, though I can't see why she'd want to make it appear to be murder or why she'd implicate me. I'm picturing myself in a cell unless something sends the police on another track." At that time arrest, humiliating as it would be, seemed the worst possible scenario. Why is it we never see the really bad things coming?

There was news on the publishing front. My helpful eldest had done as she'd promised and buttered up her friend the author. "He was kind of snooty about it," said the girl who can snoot with the best of them when she pleases. "He asked if you were a member of any writers' associations. When I made one up, he said he'd help you out."

"Rachel!"

"Now he can tell his agent you're worth a look, since someone somewhere had you fill out a form. That's how these things are done. You didn't really think people get published by being good writers, did you?"

I had at one time, but I wasn't about to admit to something so patently dumb. "Anyway, he'll speak to his agent, and you can send her a query and the first three chapters. You have got three chapters that are ready for submission, haven't you?"

"Just about."

"Keep writing. I absolutely have to attend a conference on Saturday, since I'm the speaker, but I'll leave right afterward and be there sometime Sunday morning. We'll see what old Hunky Bates can do with both of us pushing him."

Though I'd insisted I didn't need her to come home, Rachel's statement lifted a weight from my neck as big as a barbell. I hadn't told Tony, who was currently in Japan, about my problem. It would only worry him, and what could he do?

Still, I needed support right now, and I felt a rush of gratitude for Rachel, who'd sensed it and responded.

"I'm dying to talk with this Sergeant Dean. Sarah writes some letter then disappears in circumstances that assure you'll be blamed for it? I think she's lost it entirely."

My thought exactly, but I played devil's advocate. "Sarah may have gone weird, but criminal? The woman won't use a handicap stall in a rest room because it wouldn't be right."

"That's true. Besides being terrified of getting in trouble, it's hard for me to imagine she could successfully fake her disappearance. Still, she did steal your book."

"I thought about that, and I made myself read the whole thing. She changed details, characters' names, little things. Knowing Sarah, she's convinced herself the changes make it her work."

Rachel snorted in an unladylike manner. "The woman has a knack for self-delusion. She's been practicing for years."

"Rachel!"

"Mom, James told me once that his dad told his mom he'd spent the night at the car dealership because there was word that a ring of car thieves from Detroit was coming to steal his inventory." She snorted again. "What gang would travel that far to steal Marv's second rate, second hand cars with the odometers altered?"

"Well—" I began before I could stop myself."

"He lied, Mom. She believed him because she wanted to."

"You never told me any of this, Rache."

"She's—she was your best friend, Mom. I didn't criticize her because you got along so well."

"And now people are saying I did away with her," I moaned, coming back to the problem at hand.

"Grandpa always said you can't change the future by worrying about it, right?"

"Yes."

"Then instead of worrying, write the best query letter in the world, describe your book and your background, and email it to me. Once you've done that, get those first three chapters proofed and spiffy. We'll tell the agent it runs about 90,000 words."

"I've only got a fraction of that!" I wailed.

"Lie about it," Rachel said grimly. "Have you got the plot outlined so you know where it's going?"

"Yes, but it's hard to know until I actually do the writing

if it's going to work out the way it does in my head. Things changed in the first book as it went along."

"Try to keep it close. We'll send the sample with the query after I've looked it over and done what critiquing I can. I'm emailing you the agent's name and address. Don't forget to mention Rich Sawyer. He's going to recommend you, but you'll need to remind her."

"Rachel, I don't know if I can do this now."

"You have to, Mom. Keep in mind you're saving your reputation and your sanity at once. You're going to need to work full-time on the manuscript in case the agent wants a complete."

"In case?" I said, sounding whiny even to my own ears.

"You know there's no guarantee, even with a referral," Rachel cautioned. "Have you got vacation time?"

"Ten days, maybe."

"Take it. Write. Don't think about Sarah. Don't think about being a suspect. You can't control that, but you can write."

I promised I'd try, but my voice reflected uncertainty. Ignoring my mood, Rachel rang off with a final reminder to make the query good. I shut off the phone, unwilling to talk to anyone else, and spent the rest of the evening on the manuscript. I went to bed around ten, hoping tomorrow would somehow end this whole mess.

The morning brought no news, so I went to work on the query letter that should have been foremost in my mind but wasn't. I sat staring at my blank document screen for a few minutes then wrote: *Dear Ms. Cappechio:* I changed that to a more modern *Attention: Amy Cappechio: Richard Sawyer was kind enough to recommend me to you. Therefore I have taken the liberty of enclosing—*

It already sounded pompous and pretentious. Forcing myself to try again, I typed, *Rich Sawyer, one of your clients—*

"She knows he's her client, you burbling idiot!" I said aloud. "I'd rather write three novels than one query letter!"

At 8:00 I took a few minutes to call the clinic and inform Debbie I needed a week off. She was dying to ask me why, but I didn't let her. I was chipper, definite, and quick, and the call was over before she had a chance to slip in a question.

Imagining the busy clinic brought to mind my visit to the hospital and my meeting with the accident-prone twins. Odd that their mother was connected to the real-life events I'd used in my book. She'd spoken fondly of her brother Pete, who I now knew was the man found shot to death in the woods. Oskar suspected he'd been in on the Bay View robberies.

Out of curiosity I googled Angela Barr and found a phone number. If I called her, what would I say? "Do you know anything about your brother's death you didn't tell the police?" Or how about, "Can you explain why my best friend disappeared and implicated me in the process?"

I'm not sure why, but I made the call. A kid answered. I had no idea which twin it was, couldn't have said if they were standing in front of me. "Is your mom there?"

"Yeah, but she's sleeping," the voice said. "Can I take a message?"

That ignited a synapse. "Is she running the bar now?"

"Yeah, who is this?"

"Caroline Batzer. We talked at the hospital the other day."

"Tim almost had to go again yesterday." He chuckled. "He fell off his skateboard."

"How did that happen?"

"We were doing some stunts at the park, and he tried to grind the handrail. He almost made it."

I don't know much about skateboarding, but I know which part of the anatomy usually gets hurt when a handrail slide doesn't work out. Tim might never have kids to carry on the daredevil tradition. "I'm really sorry to hear it."

"He's okay, but he sure sounded funny when it happened."

"Listen, I don't want to bother your mom. Can you tell me if a woman named Sarah Leigh has been to see her lately?"

"No."

"No she hasn't or no you don't know?"

"I don't know."

"What time does your mom usually get up?"

"I could let you talk to Russ. He's awake."

Russ. That was the name Oskar had mentioned, the criminal type he suspected of the burglaries. Now what was I supposed to do? It served me right for acting without thinking.

"No, thanks." Now what? Tell the kid to forget my name? "I'll—um, I'll call back later."

I hung up, a little apprehensive. With all the excitement in that household, maybe Tom wouldn't remember my call.

Telling myself it was useless to fret over the fact that Russ Ranett was living at Angie's, I once again turned to the computer and my query letter. In half an hour it was good but not yet great. My writing comes in layers. Later today, faults would be apparent to me that were invisible at this moment, and I would fix them.

Pleased with that accomplishment, I went to work revising, editing, and generally improving the pages destined for the agent. I liked my heroine, liked the characters who surrounded her, and felt the murderer was engaging and sinister enough to make readers want to find out his (or her) identity. I satisfied myself the plot outline would hold up pretty well, then emailed Rachel the first three chapters in temporarily final form. That done, I continued the draft.

Writing really does make me forget everything else once I get going, and I didn't think the rest of the morning about Sarah Leigh or my possible arrest. At noon I watched the local news. No sign of Sarah yet. Rachel called, sensing I needed frequent infusions of confidence, and I relayed their vague report that the police were investigating a "possible crime." Still, everyone in Abaletta knew Sarah was missing, presumed dead, and I was the person with opportunity, means, and motive to do her harm.

"I have to admit, I'd look guilty to me," I told Rachel as I dug in the refrigerator for something to call lunch. I found a tomato and some mayonnaise and decided on a tomato sandwich. Bread and butter were the only other ingredients necessary, and I was sure I had those. "If she did steal my book, I killed her for it, and if she didn't, I'm obviously a jealous nut case who can't handle my friend's success."

"Hang on, Mom. There's a lawyer in Petoskey who sounds capable. He's in court today, but he promised to contact you tomorrow."

It felt good to have someone step in and share the decision-making, something I hadn't had since Ben died. I pride myself on being independent, but no one wants to face being a murder suspect alone. I wrote feverishly all afternoon and slept better that night, telling myself that any day without an arrest was a good one.

Chapter Sixteen

The next morning found me still enthusiastic about the novel, a good sign since it's hard to write when I have to force myself. The plot was racing along when the doorbell rang, and I leaned back in my chair to peer out at the porch. I would ignore a news reporter or nosy acquaintances dying to discuss my situation.

Marv Leigh stood unsteadily at my door, looking like a caricature of himself. His pants were deeply pleated across the front, his shirt didn't match his suit, and the tie was even worse. His hair stood up at the crown, and he hadn't bothered to shave. Marv needs to do that daily lest he scare the very young and the faint of heart.

Hurrying to the door, I said, "Please, come in."

"Can't," he said, shaking his head like a fly-plagued horse. "Have to go in to work."

I might have argued that nobody's work needs them in the condition Marv was, especially on a Saturday. The smell of stale beer wafted my way when he spoke.

"I think Sarah's alive," he announced. "I think she called last night."

Relief began to flood my mind, but I pushed it back. Marv

had said 'I think' twice. "Tell me about it." He looked around suspiciously, and again I invited him inside. "We don't have to talk on the porch."

"I've got to go," he said, but he stepped into the foyer with a glance behind him, as if someone might be watching. "Last night, maybe this morning—sometime—the phone rang. I didn't get to it right away. I was asleep."

Or passed out.

"Anyway, when I got there, I picked it up, and I said 'Hello', and there was nothing."

This was his call from Sarah? Nothing on the other end of the line? "Marv, it could have been a wrong number, or the person gave up, thinking you weren't home."

His red-rimmed eyes finally met mine. "When I answered there were beeps, like those back-up alerts on big trucks. It was in the background, but I'm sure that's what it was. I heard a noise and a gasp, like someone was surprised, and the connection cut off. It was Sarah, Caroline. You don't live with someone all these years without being able to recognize stuff like that."

Living with someone does make small things they do recognizable, from gestures to the way they sneeze. I'd always been able to tell when my father was in church by the sound of his breathing in the hush of meditation.

"You're sure it was Sarah?"

Marv's face showed hope. "I knew you'd believe me."

"Did you tell the sheriff?"

Marv huffed a negative. "I'm pretty sure Bates thinks I did something to her. Besides, she didn't say anything." His eyes narrowed, challenging me. "But it was her."

Interesting. While I'd been dealing with Sergeant Dean's suspicions, Marv was convinced he was Bates' prime suspect. If he was innocent, it must be doubly troubling to face the prospect of his wife's death and his own arrest.

I had a moment's pity for Marv. He was suppressing some emotion with all that alcohol. I supposed he loved his wife as much as he was capable of loving outside himself. Marv would never have believed he'd lose Sarah, and facing life without her was a shock he'd have done a lot to avoid.

And now a call in the night had given him hope. It wasn't much, but I encouraged Marv to contact the sheriff as soon as he got to work and tell him about the call. Agreeing reluctantly, he shuffled toward his car. Though he was in no shape to be at work, he might be better off there than sitting at home adding more booze to his bloodstream.

Watching Marv back out of the driveway with reasonable accuracy, I glanced at the clock. I had to get to the post office, which is open so briefly on Saturdays I wonder why they bother. Pulling on shoes and a jacket, I ran a brush through my hair, noting it was time for a haircut, and left the house.

A small-town post office is a social hub. Each morning, people who aren't expecting anything the least bit exciting trek down there to wait impatiently for the employees to finish putting letters in the boxes. Their incoming mail might not be much, but it's theirs, and they want it as soon as possible.

Heaven help us if the wrong envelope shows up in a box, and at least a dozen customers a day forget their combination or can't make it work. Our patient staff manages to keep smiling most of the time, but if that's how it is everywhere, it's no wonder the phrase "going postal" has become part of the language.

One of the daily denizens is Bobby Banning, who will be chosen to personify Ne'er-Do-Well if it's ever officially designated a syndrome. Bobby looks like he's smuggling basketballs in and out of the post office under a very old, very unattractive Hawaiian shirt. He's conspicuous for his insistence the mail be sorted and boxed by nine a.m. If for some reason it isn't, he will have a comment.

Today the post office wasn't on Bobby's bad side. When I entered, the mail had been sorted and Bobby was bent over his mailbox, face inches from the dial as he mouthed the numbers of his combination. It's hard to miss that wide a rear, and the pants were the same shapeless green Dickies he always wears. My plan was to slip by unnoticed, but he turned, his hands full of junk mail, and spotted me.

"Miz Batzer, I was just talking to someone about you."

Yeah, I'll bet. "Good morning, Bob."

"Terrible about Miz Leigh, ain't it?"

"Yes." *Minimal responses, maybe he'll give up.*

"She's a good lady, that Sarah Leigh, even if she overdoes it sometimes."

No good response to that one. "Umm."

Bobby rattled on in typical fashion, oblivious to my lack of enthusiasm. "I would never speak ill of the d—of someone who isn't here, but she makes some people mad."

I couldn't help but show a bit of interest. Someone other than me who might have a grudge was interesting. "Really."

Bobby's eyes lit like a fisherman with a nibble on the hook. "Yeah, my neighbor had a set-to with Miz Leigh last summer."

I tried to ignore Bobby's body odor as he leaned toward me confidentially. "Adeline, she spanked her son. Now she didn't beat him or nothing, but she walloped him good with a switch 'cause he trampled her roses going after a baseball."

The crowd of three in the vestibule listened intently, and there was a surge of reaction, some deeming the punishment correct and others horrified by it. Bobby warmed to his audience.

"Well, Rodney, that's the kid, he went in to get a haircut the next day. He kinda cringed when he sat down, and Miz Leigh got out of him how he got spanked." Bobby wiped his nose on his sleeve. "Now bruises on a kid's butt don't hurt him permanently, and Rodney needs discipline if a kid ever did. But Miz Leigh, she got all upset and told Adeline if she ever touched that boy again she'd get the authorities after her. Can you believe that? Her own son, and she isn't allowed to make him behave. That Miz Leigh's a funny lady."

One of the listeners remembered Sarah was missing. "She didn't deserve to get drowned, though."

"Oh, no, no, 'course not," Bobby assured us. "I just thought it was funny a woman who's usually so nice got all mad and told old Adeline off."

I could have commented on the story. If a kid was involved, Sarah would be fearless. Her love for children was obvious in her expression, in the unconscious reaching gestures she made toward any infant that came into view, in her service to the school and the town. If an event made the world a better place for kids, Sarah was all for it.

Unwilling to take the subject of Sarah's disappearance up with Bobby and the others who were watching to see what I'd say, I excused myself. Their eyes watched my back as they wondered what I knew about it.

The woman behind the counter, who amazes me with her recall of names and addresses in the area, was clearly dying to talk about Sarah too, but she held on to her professional manner, sticking to the proscribed, "Do you need insurance or confirmation on that?" I stayed businesslike as I asked for their speediest service.

It was my day for Leighs, for when I left the post office, I almost ran into James, the last person I wanted to see. James Leigh brought the word *punk* to mind, and not in the musical sense. Smaller than average, he always looked like someone had just finished shaking him by his shirtfront. His hair was a mess before it was fashionable to have it so, and his expression seldom lightened above a glare. When he saw me, the glower got several shades deeper.

"James," I said, aware of the curiosity of half of Abaletta behind me. "Any news?"

I'd always tried to be good to Sarah's oldest, sensing a tortured soul inside that surly persona. I thought James liked me as much as he was capable of liking anyone. Besides, he's not one for bold confrontations, at least when he's sober.

The only response I got was a muttered negative.

Pulling him aside so we weren't overheard, I said, "I'm sorry your mother is missing. I'm praying she's all right and will be back with us soon."

His expression was hard to read, but I thought I saw both fear and anger. "I didn't do nothing to nobody!" With that he pushed his way past me and went on.

James' comment hinted at guilt, and as he went on in his unique strut-slouch, I wondered briefly if he'd had anything to do with Sarah's disappearance. Possible scenarios included an angry fight over money or his anti-social behavior. No matter the cause, I couldn't see James hurting Sarah. She was his anchor and always had been. He'd never hurt her.

Unless it was an accident.

Back at home I sat down at my computer, but this time it was hard to immerse myself in the story. As far as violent tendencies went, James was the most likely cause of Sarah's disappearance. But he also had a lot to lose if Sarah wasn't around. She was his sometime financial support, anytime baby-sitter, and staunch defender, no matter what he did wrong.

Setting thought of James aside, I returned to Marv's visit. Had the call he received been from Sarah? Had Marv received any call at all? He was pretty much a wreck. If he had, it could have been a wrong number. The beep in the background was interesting, though. There were lots of those beeping vehicles around, but it was unusual to hear them at night. Had it been night, or was Marv mistaken about the time?

Unable to make a decision with so little to go on, I forced myself to put the newest bits of my real-life puzzle at the back of my mind. There was much to do in the land of fictional mystery, and there, at least, I controlled the story.

By two o'clock my back ached from bending toward the computer, always a problem for wearers of bifocals. The story had again begun to move along well. There's nothing like a deadline to get me going, and this was a big one. If I didn't demonstrate my talent, I'd be a laughingstock. Of course, proving myself the author created a motive: revenge on the woman who'd stolen my first book.

I was getting a snack to rest my fingers and reward myself when the phone rang. It was Damon Bates, and I was embarrassed to be caught with a mouthful of peanut butter cookie.

"Caroline?"

"Yeth?"

"I've got two bits of news. The good part is you have an alibi for the time of Mrs. Leigh's disappearance."

"I do?" I swallowed a quick sip of iced tea and washed the dry crumbs down my throat. "I mean, what do you mean?"

He actually chuckled at my confusion. "A disinterested party confirms you were in all that afternoon. He saw you come home, even saw you doing laundry."

"Someone was watching me?"

"Sergeant Dean is almost sulking," he said with a touch of humor. I guessed Damon's human side had been awakened by his dislike for Dean's open-and-shut viewpoint. "One of your neighbors called in. He's temporarily incapacitated, so he sits in front of his window all day. He can see directly into your house."

Abner Southwell, who lives kitty-corner from me, had broken his leg in a fall and was immobilized in one of those awful contraptions that screw into your very being. Seeing into my house would require high-powered binoculars, but I wasn't about to complain. Old Abner's version of *Rear Window* had gotten me off the hook, though I'd have to reconsider curtains.

Suddenly Damon's phrasing hit me. The good part? That meant there was bad to follow. "What's the rest?"

He paused, and I pictured him slouched in his chair. "Mrs. Leigh's granddaughter is missing."

"Oh no!"

"She picked the child up at her son's the day before she disappeared, and no one's seen her since. James Leigh was out of town until this morning, and his cell was out of minutes. He didn't know what was going on until we caught up with him."

"Why would Sarah take Spring to Shoepac Lake at this time of year?"

"I thought maybe you'd be able to help me with that." His tone held no suspicion, just a simple request from someone who knew Sarah well.

"Maybe they were on a nature hike of some kind. She's always showing Spring things to stimulate her mind." Odd at this time of the year, when nature was still mostly dormant, but I had no other ideas.

I heard another line ringing in Bates' office. "Well, I thought you'd want to know."

"Thanks for the call."

"No problem." There was a pause as this man of few words considered a declaration. "I never took the idea of you doing away with Mrs. Leigh seriously."

"I appreciate that."

As I hung up, tears welled in my eyes. Not just Sarah but now Spring too, possibly dead. I remembered the last time I'd seen the child, clinging to her grandmother's leg as Sarah talked with someone in the grocery store. She'd been dressed in blue, because everything Sarah bought for her was blue. Though perhaps lacking in imagination, Grandma had nevertheless seen the child's advantage. Dark eyes, dark hair, and pale skin made Spring an arresting child, not beautiful but impossible to ignore. Sarah's pride in other people's admiration for her grandchild had been almost painful to watch.

Many of us try to atone via grandchildren for our perceived failings of the past. Grandparents spend hours with tots, patiently showing them how to plant a flower or bake a cake, because during their own children's growth years, life was a blur of "go here" and "do that." If Sarah felt she'd failed James in some way, she was determined Spring would have all her attention. It was like her to take the blame for her son's quirks on herself and work twice as hard to make life perfect for his child.

Suddenly I remembered Marv's visit, his insistence that Sarah was alive. Picking up the phone, I called the sheriff back. "Did Marv Leigh call you this morning?"

"Not that I know of, why?"

"He stopped by here claiming he'd had a call from Sarah. She didn't speak, but he swears it was her." The story sounded weak as I said it. "He seemed sure, but if she called, where is she?"

There was a pause as Damon again decided how much he was willing to say. Honesty won out, but he phrased his answer carefully. "Sometimes a person wants to be missing for a while, maybe to make people appreciate her a little more. But once it's under way, everyone goes into a panic. The police get involved, the community is shocked. All that goes right along with a disappearance."

"Like the runaway bride or a kid who claims he was abducted by a big scary man?"

"It happens. After a while the person wants to come home and forget the whole thing. Of course, that's not possible."

"You mean—"

"Caroline, I'm talking when I shouldn't here, but I've known you for a while. Sarah had no cause to write that letter, did she?"

"No. She's been upset with me, but I've never figured out why. I certainly never threatened her. I was more hurt than mad."

Damon had said as much as he would about an ongoing case. "Okay. I'll be in touch, and I'll check with Marv on the call."

Chapter Seventeen

I went back to the computer, but my muse had deserted me. Though cleared of suspicion, I couldn't stop fretting over what had happened to Sarah and that darling little girl. Damon Bates seemed to think Sarah was hiding from the world for some reason, but what about the scene at the lake? I was sick at the thought of harm coming to either Sarah or Spring.

My thoughts returned to James. There were only two people in the world who cared about him, his mother and his daughter, and both of them were missing. No wonder he'd looked like a wreck.

In twenty minutes I was on my way to his home with a couple dozen warm cookies in a disposable tin. Whenever I make cookies, I bake a few and freeze the rest of the dough. It allows for fresh baked goods in no time at all, and while they don't change a thing, cookies are the best comfort food ever.

James lives in a trailer at the end of one of Abaletta's less attractive streets. The houses along the way are shabby at best, disgusting at worst. James' trailer was better than some, but not by much. A lawnmower sat at one side of the yard, apparently where it had broken down the summer before.

The trailer showed signs of decay and neglect. The exterior light was on though it was mid-afternoon, its shade cracked and slightly askew. A rough porch had been constructed from 2x4s at the front door, and toys littered it and the ground below. Most of them had been out in the weather until their bright colors faded to pastel. A pair of extremely dirty, wet socks hung over the porch rail, a muddy pair of jeans beside them. The only interest James seemed to hold onto in life was dirt-bike riding, and it appeared he'd been mud-bogging recently.

I knocked on the door. There was a long wait, and I saw the blinds move as someone looked to see who was outside. About the time I thought he wouldn't answer the door, James appeared, the scowl still in place.

"James, I just heard about Spring. I'm so sorry." I stopped when a woman appeared behind him.

Not that a woman at James' house was surprising. Abaletta has its share of misguided females who believe they can save men like James, so he was seldom without companionship. Whatever rescue response he engendered in the local women never ran very deep or lasted very long.

This woman was no tag-home from the bar though. She

wore the uniform of the Michigan State Police, blue jacket and pants with a hat tucked under her left arm, and her purpose was obviously business. She had that striking blue eye color that comes only from contacts. Her face was thin, with a little too much makeup for a cop but expertly done, and her short hair was perfectly arranged into soft curls. Her posture was more than usually erect, as if she practiced.

I noticed her black low-quarters a little smugly. My shoe size is big enough that I appreciate knowing there are attractive women out there with larger feet than mine.

"This is Officer Eckley, with the State Police. She's looking into—" James couldn't put a name to it and ended lamely—"things. Caroline's a friend of my mother's," he explained. Interest flickered in the woman's eyes, and she examined me critically. I wished I'd at least run a brush through my hair, which was probably a mess from the unconscious mauling I give it as I type.

"Hello," I said. "Sheriff Bates just told me about Spring. I hope you find them both safe."

"We hope so too." Her tone was flat, as if she was tired of well-wishing citizens. If she'd had children of her own, she'd have been more sympathetic. "I'm sure you've been asked if you know anything that will help our investigation."

"Yes." I didn't mention I used to be Suspect #1.

"I have a few additional questions." The woman's manner was professional but just a little Hollywood. She seemed as taken with the television version of cops as most of the nation apparently is.

"I told Sheriff Bates everything I know."

Her expression remained blank, but the disdain in her voice couldn't be disguised. "We don't necessarily share everything we're thinking with the local constabulary."

I resented the sneer at Damon, and she sensed it. Shifting her feet and her manner, Eckley began again. "Is it true Ms. Leigh did not write *Murder on a Vacant Property*?"

I sneaked a look at James, whose scowl got even deeper. "Could we talk about this privately?"

Eckley asked James to excuse us in a tone that indicated he had no choice in the matter. The two of us walked out into the front yard, where a sad-looking trike lay turned on its side, the plastic ribbons on the handlebars flopping softly in the breeze. Clouds had gathered in the sky, looming a warning of spring storms.

"*Murder on a Vacant Property* is my work," I told Eckley when we were alone. "I can't prove it, but it is."

"Did you know Peter Miltowski?"

"No. He was dead by the time I ever heard of him."

"You never spoke with him here in Abaletta."

"No."

"Miltowski knew this area, and we've reason to believe he may have hidden stolen goods here."

Something tickled the back of my brain, like the brush of an insect's wings, and then floated away. "What has that got to do with me, or with Sarah's disappearance?"

"We don't know." Eckley's eyes narrowed. "So neither you nor Ms. Leigh knew the people involved in the crimes you described in the book?"

"No. I made up the part about the guy coming to Abaletta."

Eckley regarded me carefully for a moment. "Thank you for your assistance."

Turning abruptly, she returned to the trailer, where James slumped resentfully in the doorway. Handing him a business card she said, "Mr. Leigh, don't hesitate to call my cell if you think of anything more I should know."

James mumbled something. Eckley made her way across the yard, still lumpy from the winter thaw, and clipped off down the street, since there was no sidewalk. I wondered briefly where she'd left her car. Maybe her partner—Dean, I guessed—had dropped her off and gone to canvass the neighbors.

I stepped onto the porch again, where James was watching the cop disappear. First I told him I'd been cleared of suspicion in his mother's disappearance. It didn't make him any friendlier. He took the plate of cookies from me with no thanks, as if they were his due. Like his father, I reflected: providing for men is what women are supposed to do. While I resented the implication, I obviously bought into it or I wouldn't have brought along baked goods.

"What do the police say about Spring?"

"They don't know anything. Some of her stuff was in Mom's car, but that's no surprise. No sign of her at the lake though." He showed no grief. James' emotions come in bursts, anger and joy flaring quickly before subsiding into apathy. His daughter was missing, his mother might have drowned, and James was wolfing down cookies as if he might never in his life get another one.

I got little else from the visit except the feeling I'd done what I could for James. He recalled nothing unusual about Sarah when she'd picked up the child, though he said she'd been "real grumpy" lately.

"What do you mean by that?"

His flat face closed and his eyes dropped to the cookies. "You know how she gets. Telling me how I should do stuff."

I gathered Sarah might have commented on the state of his house, which was deplorable. Dirty dishes were stacked everywhere, shiny, colorful boxes that had once held microwavable meals were strewn around the stove and countertop. I was surprised Sarah hadn't cleaned the place herself. It would drive her crazy to have Spring living in this mess, and I guessed James counted on her to clean it up periodically.

"She wanted me and Spring to move back home."

I applauded that idea, if only to protect the child from ptomaine. "Did you agree?"

He frowned. "We do okay. It ain't pretty, but the kid gets fed." James brooded for a moment on things he left unsaid. "Kids fall down. She wasn't hurt or nothing."

It felt as if James spoke not to me but to his mother, and his tone was defensive. Had Sarah accused him of mistreating his daughter? James was a coward, and cowards often vent their rage on those who can't oppose them. It was awful to think of a child growing up that way.

Then I remembered: Spring might already be dead, drowned in Shoepac Lake by some unknown person. Once more I considered the possibility James had done away with his own mother and child. It just didn't work for me. Neither James nor Marv would intentionally harm the woman who enabled them to live their lives in the way they preferred.

Unless there was something I had no inkling of yet.

I went home, sure that concentrating on my book would be impossible with the real-life mystery that now surrounded me. As I feared, my plot did not thicken, so I contented myself with proofing what was done, catching some things over-explained and others neglected. When the phone rang I answered it automatically, not realizing for a moment there was no response to my hello. Pushing back from the keyboard and rolling my neck to release the tension, I repeated, "Hel-lo-o!"

"Caroline?" Sarah's voice sounded very far away and tinny, like she was speaking through a culvert pipe.

My first reaction was relief. She was alive! "Sarah, where are you? Everyone's frantic with worry."

"Can you come for me? I got out, but I need a ride."

I'll admit to a moment of rebellion. Sarah had rejected me and implicated me in her supposed murder. Now I was supposed to rush to her aid? And "got out" of what? An alien spaceship that had abducted her for weird experiments? "Tell me where you are, and I'll send Sheriff Bates."

"No! They'll hurt Spring if I go to the police."

Spring was alive, then, though possibly in danger. I reminded myself Sarah wasn't acting rationally. "The police are already involved, Sarah. They're looking for you."

"But if I call them from home and tell them I'm okay, it will be better. I need to do it this way, Caro."

What right did she have to even call me, much less make this whiny request? Part of my mind said this was the moment to tell her how much she'd hurt me over the past two years. It was time for paybacks, to leave her to get out of the mess she'd made by herself, just as she'd gotten in. Instead I heard myself saying, "Where are you?"

"At a cabin near Shoepac Lake but back in the woods."

Typically for northern towns in Michigan, Abaletta has cabins scattered unevenly all over its outlying areas. Most are on lakes and rivers, and sometimes they're so close to each other you could touch the wall of one from the window of another. But plenty of them sit isolated too: hunting camps, fishing cottages, and getaway shacks in the middle of nowhere with no running water, no electricity, and no amenities.

"Which cabin?"

"You know the road to the landfill?"

"Yeah." Marv's claim of beeping trucks made sense now.

"I'm at a cabin to the south of it. There's a side road that isn't marked, but you and I went down it picking berries a few times. Do you remember a lane where the bushes grow right up to the road? The cabin's at the end, cedar siding and a log roof."

"I think I can find it. Why are you out there?"

"I'll explain when you get here. Please hurry!"

"Okay. I'm on my way."

The call started breaking up, and her last transmission came through in desperate bits. "Don't—anyone, Caro— please. Just—and—me."

I hung up without answering, irritated with Sarah and myself. Why couldn't I say no when I had all the reasons in the world to do so? First I was a danger to Sarah and now I was supposed to be her savior? It was all wrong.

It did cross my mind that this was some sort of setup, but

I'd known Sarah for a very long time. There was real tension in her voice, and she was back to her old self, depending on me to lead. But once I got her home, what then?

Damon Bates had probably been correct. In her desire to have it be so, Sarah imagined if she returned home and said her disappearance was a misunderstanding, it would all go away. How would she explain the abandoned car, the note, my sweater left as a damning clue? I pictured her calmly insisting everyone had made irrational assumptions based on incomplete observations. With the conviction Sarah could display that she was correct, she might even get away with it.

As I got into the car, I noticed that angry clouds blocked the whole sky, layer after layer growing darker as they piled against each other. The temperature was cool but not cold, and I was grateful for that. Though our snow was gone, there's always a chance of one more dose, Mother Nature's way of letting us know who's in charge. Rain tonight for sure, and it didn't look like a shower. I promised myself when I got there I'd sit in the car and let Sarah come to me. I wasn't going to get wet on her account when those looming clouds let go.

Chapter Eighteen

I covered the eight miles on the main road quickly then turned east. The road to Shoepac Lake is graveled, and it was as deserted as tertiary roads around Abaletta usually are, except during high summer. I slowed for the three miles of washboard I knew it would be after spring rains and before the county prettied it up for tourist season. The road was cut from the pine woods and had no shoulders, lots of curves to by-pass marshes and lakes, and plenty of wildlife to watch for. I met only one local denizen, a coyote that hurried into the scrub brush, embarrassed at being caught out in the daylight.

Small brown-painted signs provided by the DNR pointed along gravel roads and two-tracks, indicating local spots of interest: the Shoepac Lake campground, the Tomahawk floodwaters, several boat launches and hiking trails. Ignoring them, I continued along the gravel road to where Sarah and I had picked huckleberries in happier times. As young mothers we used to drive out here and set up shop. Soon our children would be asleep on a blanket, another blanket hung in a tree to shield them from the sun while we picked. There'd been a steady stream of chatter (at least on my part) and a friendly competition as to whose bucket got full faster with fewer "extras": leaves, bugs, and twigs. I knew what had happened to the berries, but what had happened to those carefree young mothers?

Three miles down, a turn took me onto a winding lane canopied with tree branches in summer but open now to the darkening sky above. Once I'd made the last turn, I remembered seeing the cabin. Set back about forty feet from the road and unabashedly shabby, it was small, probably one room. From the looks of it, no improvements had been made since it was built in the 1950s.

Places near the lake had probably been checked in the search for Sarah, but it would have been difficult to find them all. Besides, Sergeant Dean's conviction she was in the lake might have taken precedence over other ideas.

This cabin was about as remote as it could get, and the general emptiness of the yard suggested long disuse. I pulled in alongside the building, noting the door at the side. As I considered whether to honk the horn or just wait in the car, Sarah Leigh stepped out from behind some trees, looking frightened, rumpled, and miserable.

Jumping out of the car, I hurried toward her. "Sarah, what's going on?"

I think she wanted to hug me, but she was probably unsure whether I'd hug back or smack her. "Caro, I've made such a mess of things!"

"Indeed you have!" The voice came from behind me, and I spun around. A man stood behind my car, and the first thing I noticed was the gun he held. They say a witness will exaggerate the size of a firearm pointed at her. To me that barrel looked like a cannon's mouth.

Behind the gun was a slight man with blond, straight hair that seemed to have slid backward a few inches, elongating his forehead. His face was almost pretty: round, blue eyes, skin feminine in its smoothness and clarity, and delicate bone structure. Its only drawback was a chin that could have used both rounding and breadth.

He looked like someone I knew, maybe someone I'd seen at the clinic. The smile he affected was insincere to say the least. I would come to know it well, because it seldom left him.

Beside me, Sarah gave out a small moan of despair. The man approached and held out his hand, and reluctantly, she reached into her pocket, pulled out her cell phone, and handed it over. "Thank you." He made a mocking bow.

To make matters worse, a second man appeared from the

back corner of the cabin. This one was massive across the shoulders but small-hipped and short-legged, like the voyageurs who once canoed the Great Lakes seeking furs for trade. Dark and expressionless, he looked every bit as feral as one of those old traders closing on a deer for his supper. I felt very doe-like at that moment.

Sarah was more aware of what was going on than I. "Let her go!" she cried out. "She came to help me, but she doesn't know anything."

"She does now. She's seen us, and she's seen you." The blond man's smile never wavered, but I heard the finality in his voice. We weren't leaving that place alive.

The guy with the shoulders got into my car and drove it forward, past the cabin and into the trees until it was invisible from the road. When he got out, he casually tossed my keys into the woods, where they clattered against a tree and settled in some impossible-to-find place. Being without a vehicle was almost as upsetting to me as the gun pointed at my chest. I had no way out of there, and besides, my phone was on the seat of the car, now out of my reach.

The gun-toter ordered Sarah and me into the cabin, where I blinked for a few seconds as my eyes adjusted to the dimness. It was indeed one room, and not a large one at that.

A small casement window that faced the woods at the back was open, while a second, larger window at the front was tightly shuttered, blocking out most of the light.

It was like a lot of cabins I've been in: knotty pine walls and a cement floor covered with pieces of somebody's dingy old living room carpeting. Despite the lack of space, dusty animal heads protruded from the two windowless walls, making a gauntlet of antlers and muzzles. The furniture was a junky, eclectic mix: dilapidated chairs, a sway-backed loveseat against one wall, and bunk-beds in the opposite corner with rolled sleeping bags set atop them. A corner served as kitchen and dining area with a small table and two chairs, a hand pump and a bucket, a stand with a Coleman stove, a small shelf unit, and three grungy-looking coolers stacked against the wall for cold storage.

Scattered around the place were items associated with careless men: a dozen empty beer cans and a half-full bottle of Absolut, a stack of ancient, mismatched dishes piled in disarray and caked with the remains of several meals, and a plastic grocery bag overflowing with trash. In the center of the room an unlit lantern hung, ready to provide light in the absence of electricity. Spread out on the rickety table was a plat map of the area, its corners weighted by three rocks and an overflowing ashtray.

Gun Guy ordered us both to sit. We shared the love-seat, so musty I immediately felt the tingle of an oncoming sinus reaction. It probably wasn't worth my time to explain to Gun Guy that I wouldn't be able to sit long on the thing without having a sneezing fit.

"What's this all about?" I asked.

Gun Guy didn't even look at me. "Shut up."

The other man came in with some rough boards, and they went to work closing up the smaller window by fastening the boards over the space in an *X* shape. For a few moments there was only the sound of their pounding and a few swear words when the rocks they were using as hammers failed as effective tools.

I turned to Sarah, who seemed okay for someone whose body they were dragging the lake for at this moment. There was a raw scrape, not deep but large, on her arm, and she looked like she'd rolled in dirt. Her pale blue eyes drooped with fatigue despite the fear in their depths. If she'd been held prisoner since she went missing, where had the staged drowning scene that implicated me come from? Why had she written the letter that accused me? And if she was a prisoner, how had she managed to call first Marv and then me?

When the second window was covered, Gun Guy pulled up a rickety chair and sat down across from us, the gun resting loosely in one hand. "I'da never believed a full-grown woman could get out that window," he said to Sarah. "You left some hide on the edges, didn't ya?"

When Sarah stared straight ahead, no expression on her grime-streaked face, he scratched at a mosquito bite on his neck. "We got back just in time. And where'd you get that phone? I know I searched you good."

Sarah spoke without looking at him. "It was in my jacket."

"That's why you were so anxious to get it out of your van before we left the lake, huh?" His mouth twisted in rueful afterthought. "I shoulda checked the jacket too."

We sat silently for a while, waiting for something. Finally the second man returned to the cabin, wiping his feet at the door from some leftover trace of childhood teaching. "Nobody else around, Russ."

Russ! My jaw clenched when I heard the name, and I cursed my own stupidity. I should have called Damon despite Sarah's plea, or at least left word with someone where I'd gone. Now we were miles from assistance. From the end of snowmobile season until the huckleberries come out in July, the plains around Abaletta are populated mostly by deer, elk, and jackrabbits.

"What now?" Shoulders asked.

"That depends on the ladies," Russ replied. "*A*, they tell us where our stuff is, we let them go and we're on our way. *B*, they don't, in which case we get upset, and something bad could happen." Shoulders twitched uncomfortably but said nothing.

"We can't tell you anything," Sarah said in a flat tone. "We don't know." It sounded like they'd been through this before.

Russ grinned. "Your memory might improve now your friend is here." Looking at the other man, he said in a tone that was hardly suggestion, "Why don't you bring in that 12-pack, Zane."

Without a word, the big-shouldered guy left the cabin. As soon as he was gone, Russ' blue eyes met mine. "You've got until midnight. If one of you can't remember meeting Pete by then, I set this place on fire."

My heart sank. These men were the Bay View robbers Detective Oskar had told me about. Russ was the guy with no conscience, and Zane was probably the one Oskar conjectured had access to the houses. Apparently the fact that we knew nothing about those crimes made no difference. If Sarah or I couldn't tell them what they wanted to know, they would burn this place down with us inside.

"You can't do that." Sarah meant it to be a command, but it came out a plea.

"You'll get credit for a murder-slash-suicide, Miz Leigh. The police will conclude you called Miz Batzer out here because you had some grudge against her." He leaned toward Sarah, pointing a finger in mock severity. "And they won't be all wrong, will they?"

The man called Zane returned in time to hear the end of it, and he paused at the tone of threat. If he thought about arguing for mercy, however, he rejected it as either not worth the effort or not likely to be heeded. Setting the beer on the rickety table he took one, popped it open, and said, "I'll go get the truck."

"No hurry," Russ said. "We're going to give them some time to talk it out and decide to cooperate. One of them met Pete. One of them knows something that will help us out."

Zane shrugged and went outside. Russ took a beer for himself and followed, shooting us a grin and pointing a finger as if to say we should get to work. The door slammed behind him, and I heard something clunk against it, a brace of some kind to stop us from opening it from within.

"Caro, I'm so sorry," Sarah began in a rush as soon as he was gone. "When they left I climbed out the window, but I had no way to get back to town. I thought if you picked me up, we could be gone before they got back." She wiped her eyes with her sleeve. "I shouldn't have called you—Russ is crazy!"

"Sarah, we have about two minutes to decide what to do or we'll be dead. Is there another way out of here?"

"I don't think so."

I'd seen that myself but hoped there was something I'd missed.

"Then we'll have to surprise them."

She turned to me in confusion. "How can we do that?"

I squinted through the gloom, considering what might be useful. Antlers were great weapons for deer, but the original owners hadn't fared well against guns.

"First we need to make them think we're still sitting here when we're not," I whispered. "Get those sleeping bags and prop them up on the couch." Sarah did as I said while I collected a flashlight, a blanket, and two cast-iron pans. I spread the blanket over the back of the loveseat, draping it into what I hoped resembled two heads atop the sleeping bag "torsos." When the men came in from outside, it would take their eyes a moment to adjust to the room's dimness. Hopefully, the amorphous shapes would fool them for long enough.

"Stand behind the door and take this pan. When they're both inside the doorway, clobber whoever comes in first. I'll handle the second one. Wait until they're both inside though."

"Hit him with this?" Sarah took the pan I shoved at her, but her voice betrayed unwillingness, maybe inability, to do such a thing.

"Sarah, they're going to kill us."

It was all I had time to say, for a scrape outside indicated that the wooden brace had been removed. Footsteps sounded on the wooden pallet that served as the cabin's porch. I flattened myself against the wall, praying Sarah would follow a lifetime of habit and trust my lead.

Zane came in first, stopping in the doorway. The vague outline on the couch suggested our presence there, and he leaned toward it suspiciously for a moment before stepping inside. I held my breath, wondering if he could smell my sweat as I stood poised to attack. It took all my concentration not to act too soon, but I waited until Russ entered. "Shoulda grabbed the flashlight," he muttered.

My chest felt like it would burst, either from my pounding heart or my overextended lungs. He took a step toward the table, and, putting my weight on my back foot, I drew the pan back and struck him just over the ear as hard as I could swing. The pan made a resounding metallic gong sound, the man an accompanying grunt as he staggered sideways and fell to one knee.

Zane turned with a questioning, "Huh?" He got a glimpse of me, but that was all. Gripping the handle like a softball bat, Sarah brought her pan up, catching him under the chin and snapping his head back like a Pez doll. I wouldn't have done it that way, but the blow sent him to the floor. We stood over them, triumphant and unbelieving at the same time.

Chapter Nineteen

Not for long. Zane stirred almost immediately, and I realized this wasn't the movies, where bad guys conveniently stay unconscious while the heroes escape. "Go!" I pushed Sarah toward the door, and she responded quickly. I pulled it closed, glancing around for a brace. Seeing my purpose, Sarah picked up the board they'd used to wedge the door shut and jammed it under the knob. It wouldn't stop them, but it would slow them down.

"Now what?" she asked. "If we take the road they'll catch up before we get a mile."

"We go cross-country," I said grimly, pointing west, where the main road lay.

If you have to run through the woods of Michigan, spring isn't the best time but it's not the worst either. Bushes hadn't sprouted yet, so we passed fairly quickly, with only brittle, long-dead burrs, thistles, and thorns catching weakly at our clothing. Michigan hadn't yet hatched its full spring crop of black flies, second only to Canada's, but the blood the few existing insects might take was nothing compared to what our pursuers would exact if they caught us.

I led the way, trying to keep our direction mainly

westward though we zig-zagged to try to confuse our pursuers. Cabins sat scattered around the area, but not one of them was likely to be inhabited at this time of year. No lights shone anywhere to guide us, and we floundered through the dark woods clumsily, trying to keep quiet but unable to. I was afraid to use the flashlight I'd brought along.

Even if we weren't recaptured, a lot of bad things could happen to us. We might stumble into a bear, grumpy from his winter sleep. One of us could trip on a tree root and injure herself. Or we might blunder into one of the sinkholes and end up rolling down its steep sides, with trees and rocks to make the passage even more perilous.

Finally I whispered, "We have to hide somewhere till they give up looking for us. We're making so much noise that we're losing the advantage of the start we got on them."

It's not easy to find a place to hide in a pitch-black forest. We couldn't tell if the place we chose, a broken tree, provided enough of a screen to shield us from view if a flashlight was directed at us. Still, we had little choice. We settled in to wait, tense, frightened, and unable to swat effectively at things that crawled on us, real and imagined.

That's when the rain began. Drops started slowly here and there, one plopping on my head with a splat and then another on my hand. Within minutes there were sheets of it, drenching us and pounding the leaves where we sat half-buried into mush. Miserable as I was, I had to appreciate that the deluge made us more difficult to track, though occasional flashes of lightning lit the whole area like strobes, outlining Sarah's frightened face. I sat watching the darkness, tensing at every lightning strike. In front of me a branch dripped water steadily, and the flashes turned the drops to diamonds on a string. I watched in exhausted fascination as they came and went, each one that fell immediately replaced by a new one at the opposite end. Too tired and frightened to think, I let Mother Nature block out everything else.

Then as suddenly as it started, the rain withdrew, its roar lessening to gradually slowing snare drum beats, then stopping altogether except for sporadic, syncopated drips.

***

That's where this story began, with Sarah and I crouched in the gully and two criminals hunting the woods for us, one so near I could have whispered to him. We were lucky that March had turned mild in its middle days. Plenty of spring seasons in Michigan are too cold to survive an unexpected night outside. Still, it wasn't pleasant. We were cold, thirsty, and shaking with fear.

There's no terror like that of being hunted, unable to get away and having to wait and see if you are discovered. You want to scream, you want to cry, you want to run, but any of those things will get you killed. You force your body to remain still.

After a tense few minutes, the man nearer to us, Zane, moved off. In response we heard Russ move away too, and I saw a faint flash of light in that direction. Our first piece of luck: they had only one flashlight, and its beam didn't turn our way.

A couple of hours later, I was fairly sure they'd given up. They had a daunting task, finding two women in a huge state forest in the dead of night. Leaning toward me Sarah whispered, "We've got to get out of here."

"Why?" I whispered.

"I've got to—I've got to get somewhere."

Great! Now I had a schedule to keep as well as saving her bacon. Still, she was right. It was black night now, but if Russ and Zane came back at daylight, we'd be easily visible. There were no leaves on the tree to hide us, and Sarah's white shirt would show up like a flag against the dark branches. Even her whites were whiter than mine.

Without more discussion, we crawled stealthily from our

hole. The first thing I did was make Sarah switch her shirts around, putting her dark green turtleneck over the white shirt that stuck out so starkly in the dark woods.

"Take off my shirt? Out here?" she asked.

At her reluctance to strip down, I rolled my eyes. "As if modesty matters at this point!"

Once she obeyed I started off. My night of pondering had resulted in the decision to abandon our run for the highway and instead head east, toward the lake, where there should be a place with a working phone.

Our progress was slow and often painful, but after a while I detected a lightening of the sky ahead. At least that made east easier to find. Darkness hindered every step, and we dared not use the flashlight I still clutched. We plodded along, single file and miserable. Quiet was essential, so we held onto each other, a press of the hand signaling a pause or renewed movement. It was odd. Despite years of being friends, we had seldom touched. Now we clung to each other from both physical and emotional necessity.

That didn't stop me from wanting to smack Sarah. My feet ached, as they were wont to do since they hit middle age. I was tired, wet, starving to death. When had I eaten last? I couldn't recall lunch yesterday, might have skipped it due to working so hard on the book, which I wouldn't have had to do if Sarah hadn't stolen the first one. I wouldn't be here if she hadn't called me. Why not the sheriff? It was his job to rescue people, not mine.

Behind me I heard Sarah muttering. Actually it sounded more like spitting. "What?" I asked, wary of ears other than hers.

Gray tones showed where Sarah's cheeks, chin and forehead were, and a dark spot widened as she answered, "I said *Murder on a Vacant Property* got me into this mess. I'm cold, tired, thirsty, and wet, and I hate that stupid book."

For a moment I stood still, trying to think of something withering enough to say. How could a book be to blame for our trouble and not the person who stole it? In the end I turned and trudged on toward the pink edge showing at the base of the next rise, at a loss for words.

My watch said ten to seven when we stumbled onto the trail. It was the first sign we'd seen of civilization, though a path with a series of blue dots on the trees doesn't exactly indicate a population center. It had to be the hiking trail that circled the sink holes, which meant if we followed it we'd come to the campground. With luck, a fisherman or a ranger would show up, and we'd be saved.

The question was where we were on the trail. If we chose the wrong direction, we'd end up taking the long way, a full three-hour circle. I had no way to judge how close we were to the starting point or which direction to go.

As I stood trying to decide, a rustle to my left sent me to a crouch. Beside me Sarah followed suit, and we froze as Russ emerged from the woods not fifty feet away. He stretched, yawned, and rubbed his neck as if there were kinks in it, leading me to conclude he'd given up searching the dark for us and found a place to get some sleep. Behind him came Zane, his stoic manner undaunted by a night in the north woods. Both men looked as bedraggled as we did, which was a tiny bit satisfying. Their gazes combed the woods around them, and I fought the urge to scoot backward. Movement was likely to catch their attention, but if we remained still, I doubted they could pick us out in the jumble of branches between us and them.

They spoke in low tones, discussing the sun, just showing over the horizon. They inspected the trail and came to an agreement. Russ went off one way and Zane the other, the worst case scenario for Sarah and me.

Russ passed a few feet from where we crouched, where my legs cramped in the unnatural position they were stuck in, and where Sarah's breathing sounded like a locomotive to my ears. He heard and saw nothing, and soon he was out of sight. As she relaxed a little, I began figuring.

"We have to go through it."

"What?" Sarah knew what I meant but couldn't fathom it. Or didn't want to.

"We have to climb down the sink and come up the other side. On the trail we'll run into one of them, and if we go back through the woods we could spend days wandering around."

"Do you know how steep that is?"

Of course I did, but what was the alternative? "We've done it before."

"When we were twelve! We're not kids anymore, Caro."

"Then what do we do? Go right and catch up with Russ or left and run into Zane?"

"It isn't helping for you to be grumpy."

Who had a better right?

I moved to the rim of the sink hole. It was indeed very steep. As kids we'd relished the 20% grade, found it fun to let our feet slide through the soft sand of a washout as we half-ran, half-fell down the bank. Now the prospect brought images of broken bones, scraped shins, and loss of balance ending in an undignified, painful roll to the bottom.

I moved off the trail and over the edge, a three-foot first step down. After that it wasn't too bad for a few feet, and I turned back to see Sarah following, her lips curled under in concentration. As we made our way down it got dark again. It would be a while before the sun rose high enough to light our path.

Soon my legs protested the new adventure. Tilting my body at an awkward angle in order to remain upright on the steep slope called on muscles I hadn't used nearly enough for a decade or more. I began using tree roots as handholds to slow my progress, carefully at first for fear of poison ivy but after a while grabbing whatever could help me stay in control. Once I heard Sarah fall and felt a shower of sand on my back. She managed to stifle her yelp of pain, but we were still for a while anyway, waiting to see if Russ or Zane reacted. When we heard nothing, we continued downward.

The descent seemed to go on forever. We passed scrubby-looking jack pines, their bark encrusted with lichen and their limbs demonstrating no symmetry or grace. Interspersed along the way were oak trees, skimpy, tough-looking specimens. Clusters of long-dead leaves clung to their branches, since wind seldom reached this far down.

We followed a washout that curved around the tree trunks, leaving crazy patterns of exposed roots that at some point disappeared into the ground again. The soft sand both helped and hindered us. It was hard to keep a foothold, but in some places we slid smoothly downward at some speed, gaining distance between us and pursuit. I felt like Alice going down the rabbit hole, falling farther and farther from the world I knew and ending at a place I could only hope was better than where I'd come from.

As we neared the bottom, our descent became gentler. Thick brush blocked the way. Any similarity to Alice's gentle fall ended, and I thought instead of Sleeping Beauty's prince, hacking a path through a forest of thorns. Pulling my jacket sleeves over my hands, I raised them in front of my face like a shield and pushed through brittle branches that pulled at me and dragged painfully across any section of exposed skin.

Finally we reached level ground. I turned north, almost certain we'd come across the trailhead in that direction.

Anyone who thinks there's something interesting to see at the bottom of a sinkhole is wrong. The terrain around us looked exactly like what we'd passed through above. Trees, thick brush, and the dimness of early morning hid the steep wall we'd descended from sight, and it seemed we traversed a woods like any other as we traced the vertical line of the sink's nadir.

When daybreak finally came it was spectacular, though I was in no mood to enjoy it. Trees around us split the orange light into bands of brightness as the sun, fattening in its springtime path, appeared over the hillside above. We had all the time in the world to observe the change from dimness to full light as we trudged along. The storm had passed, and the day seemed destined to be clear. I hoped that meant warmth, for despite our brisk pace I was chilled to the bone and my clothes were still damp.

I felt it in my calves when the ground started to rise again. We'd reached the far end of the sink and now had to climb back up. We wanted to come out a hundred eighty degrees from where we'd entered. If my guess was correct that would be near the trailhead, where there was a primitive campground and familiar roads, and away from Zane and Russ. From there we'd make our way back to civilization. There was a store maybe four miles from here where they were certain to have a phone.

The climb was a nightmare. Each step up required a huge physical effort, and we grabbed at roots, tree trunks, anything that might serve as a handhold. Though we tried to be quiet, air soon wheezed through our tired lungs. Frequent rests were required, and we didn't have to discuss when we'd stop. I'd simply flop over on my back, letting my screaming arm and leg muscles relax. Sarah did the same. We might once have worried about snakes, said to lurk in the sink holes, but strain banished that fear. If a snake slithered by, so be it.

Ascent took three times as long as descent, and the sun had indeed begun warming the air as we approached the sink's rim. I listened carefully, my eyes constantly sweeping the trail above for a sign of Russ or Zane. About thirty feet to our left I saw something familiar: the DNR-installed walkway that skirted the sink, part of the hiking trail.

It was made of weatherized wood six-by-sixes, its braces sunk deeply into the ground with railings sturdy enough to allow hikers to lean out and experience the vertigo of the steep drop. In some places, jute webbing flanked the sides of the walkway to slow erosion. Benches placed at intervals along the trail gave places to rest and enjoy the view. On one such bench Russ sat, smoking a cigarette.

I put a hand back to alert Sarah, who looked up, grasped our situation, and flashed me a look of utter despair. After all our hard work, we weren't rid of them. In fact, we'd emerged in exactly the spot they'd expected us to.

Chapter Twenty

I backed down the incline until I was sure the slope hid us from Russ' line of sight. But where was Zane? If we came up somewhere else, he might be there.

"We have to skirt the sink," I whispered to Sarah. "There has to be a place where we can come out under cover."

"He'll see us," she hissed, gesturing at Russ, who gazed over the landscape before him watchfully.

"People look outward," I told her. "He won't look down very often or very long. We'll be okay if we're quiet."

They couldn't be everywhere, I reasoned as I led the way, and it had to be attempted. We began edging to the left, which was even harder going than before. Horizontally there was no path of any kind, no washouts where debris had been cleared by nature. We had to climb over branches, rocks, and clumps of disturbed detritus as we moved away from Russ and the familiar area I'd counted on for our exit.

Quiet isn't easy when you're crawling through a sinkhole. In one way last night's rain was a blessing, since damp plants are less crunchy than dry ones. Careful not to step on branches that might snap or grab dead limbs that might let go and send us toppling backward, we sidled like crabs along the sinkhole's walls, our mouths pressed closed in order to minimize anguished sounds associated with strained lungs and torn skin.

We finally exited the hole at a spot where there was no trail at all, just pines and underlying cedars growing thick enough to hide us from sight. We were much farther east than I wanted to be, since the lake was to our west. It was unfamiliar territory, and I was unsure which way to go to find a road. There were more sinkholes in the area, and I didn't want to traverse another one, ever again.

Irony is usually something I appreciate, but it didn't please me at all when Sarah, after dealing with everything she'd been through in the last few days, spoiled our efforts in an instant. As we climbed onto the rim of the sink we startled a partridge, which flew up with its characteristic drumbeat wing flutter. Someone who's never heard that sound before might be forgiven for concluding that a large beast is thundering toward her. Natives like Sarah should know better. I guess her nerves were shot, because when the bird took flight, she screamed. *Squealed* might be a better term, but it was a disastrous thing to do at that moment in time.

I heard Russ shout for Zane, and they were after us. Angrily I jerked Sarah into the woods and away from the sink, searching as we ran for a place of cover. We couldn't outrun them, so a hiding place was essential. As far as I knew there were no convenient caves in the area, and I saw no big trees to hide behind. Around us was only poplar and pine, and skinny examples at that.

The knights who rescued us weren't in armor, but their pointed weapons were impressive nevertheless. Despite the noise we were making, I heard even louder crashing in the trees off to the right. Without slowing, I stole a glance in that direction and caught a blur of movement. Large brown bodies, dark in front and pale behind, hurried away from us. Flashes of huge antlers showed through the trees as the animals laid their heads back to make their passage easier.

Elk. We had spooked a herd of at least six of them, and they were making tracks in the opposite direction. They made a terrible racket, and their panicked flight took them on a dead run directly at our enemies. The huge beasts lumbered on, unaware there were more interlopers ahead of them. I heard Russ swear in obvious panic. One five-hundred-pounder coming directly at a person would be unnerving, half a dozen had to be terrifying.

Taking advantage of our enemies' distraction, I made a turn due east, hoping they'd think we continued in a straight line. After we put as much distance between ourselves and them as we could, we took shelter under a blow-down, an old pine uprooted by a long-ago storm. If Zane and Russ didn't come directly past us, its roots would hide us from their view. Eventually they'd move on. I hoped.

When we heard nothing more for at least half an hour, I nodded to Sarah and we got to our feet. The wood was silent; both the elk and our tormentors had gone in another direction. I was exhausted. I was parched with thirst. I was hungrier than any time I could ever remember. I knew Sarah was in exactly the same shape. There was no sense discussing the situation. There was nothing to do but go on, no one to depend on but each other. Wearily, we began walking west.

At least our path was easier. We found a two-track road and followed it to a larger one, which led to a cement block structure with its door padlocked shut and its windows covered with metal mesh. I recognized the contact station for the local landfill. After all our efforts, we were less than a quarter mile from the cabin where we'd begun.

Circling the building hopefully, we found no way to get inside. The phone, visible through the window perhaps five feet away, brought me to despair after the night's terror and stress. So close.

Sarah was almost catatonic from exhaustion, but despite everything, she remained focused on a goal I didn't understand. "I need to get to Petoskey."

"We need to get out of these woods," I countered tersely.

She looked away as if listening for a voice on the breeze. "Spring's with a sitter."

Spring. I'd forgotten in the press of what was happening to Sarah and me that the little girl was missing too. She was in Petoskey? Maybe it was stress overload, but my brain refused to make sense of it. Sarah's next comment didn't clarify anything. "She's safe there. Now, let's keep moving."

"Moving where?" Ahead was the landfill, a large, flat area of buried waste covered with layers of state-demanded substances that sealed it from offending citizen sensibilities. That offered no help unless seagulls were needed.

Off to the right were several trucks. We tried the doors, but they were locked. No help.

There was the road, of course, but we feared our pursuers in that direction. A second two-track disappeared into dense brush. No telling where it went. It could lead to another sinkhole or simply dead-end a half mile down.

Sarah was staring in the opposite direction. "There used

to be a shack out here."

She was right. In the years before landfills were engineered and sanitized, people had simply dumped their trash into the deep gullies in this area and bulldozed them over when they were full. Off to one side there'd been a shed that provided shade for the attendant. If it was still there, we could hide inside until the landfill operators came to work for the day. It would be a relief to get out of sight, and even if Russ and Zane came looking, I didn't think they'd notice a tumble-down building overgrown with scrub brush.

We found the four by four structure without much trouble and forced open the weed-choked door. The only man-made item it contained was the rotted, rusty remains of one of those fifties lawn chairs with the green and white canvas cross-straps. The place had been visited over the years by every creature of the forest, and nature was well-represented with pinecones, droppings, and spider webs. Miraculously, the roof was intact and the door almost so.

"Get inside. I'll set the door in place so we're out of sight."

"There are spiders," Sarah objected. I couldn't believe that all these years I'd failed to notice how prissy she was. But then, hadn't I had to drag her, kicking and mewing, to our one and only beer party when we were in high school?

"For crying out loud, Sarah!" Taking a stick, I brushed the cobwebs out of the door frame, pushed her inside, followed, and set to work closing the door. One hinge was so rusty it broke, but when I set the door in place, it stayed put.

"I can't believe I never noticed when we were kids how bossy you are," she complained. "I remember once you made me come to some party out here and the police showed up. We almost got Minor in Possession tickets."

"Almost. And when my giving orders saves your life, you should be grateful." We lapsed into tense silence.

Once again we were in close quarters, unable to stretch out. The shack had a horizontal, fold-up shutter that opened onto the road, allowing the long-ago attendant to see cars approaching. I opened it a few inches so we could see when someone came along. We were silent for a long time, staring at the road as the sun rose higher over the trees, brightening the landscape considerably. Nothing stirred. Again I went over things, and again I couldn't see what I'd done to deserve this.

Sarah had been kidnapped, but I wasn't sure why. I'd been set up to look like a murderer, and I wasn't sure who. And if we were going to get out of this, I wasn't sure how.

With immediate terror at bay, my case of nerves twisted

to a raging anger that threatened to explode, a delayed reaction from the fear and adrenalin I'd been running on all night. "Sarah, what in hell is going on? The police think you drowned, Spring's somewhere in Petoskey, you're being chased by two guys who want to kill you, and I somehow get included by association!"

There was a long silence. I imagined Sarah pursing her lips at my language and my anger, but I would not look at her. Finally she answered meekly, "Caroline, I owe you an apology."

"You owe me about ten of them."

"I had to get Spring away. When I picked her up Tuesday morning, she had—" Sarah turned away and blinked back tears. "She had a big bruise on her cheek. James said she fell, but the marks were clearly from—" She gulped. "—knuckles."

I felt sick. James wasn't much of a father, but to hit his beautiful daughter with a fist? Realizing what she was admitting, I found I wasn't quite so mad at Sarah. She really had been pushed to the brink.

"I'm so sorry."

Surprisingly, she lashed out at me. "You have a lot to be sorry for!" I recoiled in shock as she added through clenched teeth, "James was the last straw, but I've lived in Hades for two years." Even in extreme distress, Sarah kept her language ladylike. "My best friend is no friend at all."

"Sarah, *you* turned on *me*."

Her thoughts came out garbled. "I thought when Ben died you'd fall apart. I didn't know how you kept going until he confessed. Why would I think that about my best friend?"

I picked up the bit I understood. "I did fall apart, Sarah!"

"But then you were yourself again. You had your old confidence and strength." Her eyes narrowed and the words came out in a rush. "Because you had Marv."

"Me and—" I couldn't say it, but my view cleared, like when the optometrist dials in the correct lenses. Sarah thought I'd been sleeping with her pea-brained husband.

Chapter Twenty-one

"Where in the wide world did you ever get an idea like that?" I asked.

Sarah's jaw jutted stubbornly. "Marv was just helping you get over Ben's death. It didn't mean anything to him."

So I was a pity date for the termite she had put up with for thirty years? And she believed him!

"If you had come to me with this, I'd have cleared it up right away. I thought we could talk about anything."

Her voice turned acidic, and suddenly the conversation wasn't about Marv or the supposed affair. "You talk. I listen. You never cared how I felt as long as I did what you wanted. You never once asked if I was happy."

I was stung. How had she so misunderstood my tactful avoidance of the subject of her miserable home life?

"Do you know how hard it is to be your little helper?" Sarah demanded. "To have people say how lucky you are to have good old Sarah in your shadow?"

"I never thought of it that way."

She didn't even hear me. "Then you took up with Marv. The others didn't matter, but you?"

"Marv contends that he and I—"

"He never would have admitted it, but I said I'd leave if he didn't."

"Marv never told you the truth in his life, Sarah!" I did some quick figuring. "This confession—when did it happen?"

Her face tightened with painful memories. "About two years ago. Spring's momma had left, and James—" She stopped, tried again. "I got worried about—" Sarah couldn't say what she feared, but knowing James and his low-class friends, I got it. I too had fretted about what the child might be exposed to, but I hadn't broached the issue. Sarah would be watchful, I'd told myself. It was none of my business.

The story came out slowly and with omissions, but I filled in the gaps from my own knowledge. Sarah had become so concerned for Spring that she'd considered leaving her faithless husband behind in order to remove Spring from her abusive father. It had come down to a confrontation late one night when Marv came home late, disheveled, and very drunk. Sarah had said things she'd never dared to say before.

Marv must have seen that after years of neglect, Sarah had had enough. He'd have groped for a way to appease her somehow, and with cunning typical of his type, he'd done what it took to keep his wife at home and his life the way it was.

I imagined him selling their broken marriage the same way he sold a damaged car, with diversion and misdirection. *Don't talk about the cracked cylinder, point out the nice interior.* He would have assured Sarah he'd mend his ways, help her protect Spring, and support James. He'd have played on her emotions, claiming James needed her as much as the little girl did.

Looking back, I realized it was about that time Marv had given James a mobile home he'd taken on trade, so he wouldn't have to raise Spring in the crummy apartment over the bar where he'd been living. It was also about two years ago that Marv had briefly become more attentive to Sarah. I'd seen them together a couple of times in the car, Sarah in the back, beside Spring in her car seat, while Marv drove. My thought at the time had been that I'd never seen her so happy. Apparently the bliss hadn't lasted, and knowing what I knew now, I realized it wouldn't, not with a man like Marv.

And it was about two years ago that I'd first noticed Sarah's coolness. I couldn't believe she'd fallen for Marv's lies, but she must have been pulled in so many directions she was frantic. Because she didn't know what to do, Sarah had done nothing.

Still, she'd wanted someone to blame for her inaction. In

her mind, she'd opted to fight to get the man she loved back from the evil Other Woman. Sadly, I'd had no idea I'd been appointed to the position.

When I'm angry, my arguments aren't well-presented, and I blurted out the thing uppermost on my mind. "How could you believe such a bunch of bull, Sarah? I loved Ben, and I never would have—I just wouldn't." I stopped myself from saying if I'd ever considered adultery, Marv Leigh would have been last on my list of prospects.

She looked at me as if I'd said something childish. "Sex isn't about love, Caroline. Marv always comes back to me. That's how I know he loves me."

I remembered Rachel's assessment: *The woman has a knack for self-delusion. She's been practicing for years.* Rather than admit her husband was a louse, Sarah had clung to the belief that Marv's staying with her signified not merely convenience, but true love.

"So you think I had an affair with Marv?"

Sarah's voice turned softer, less harsh. "I was spending a lot of time with Spring. I guess I neglected him."

Typically, Sarah the Enabler blamed herself for her co-dependent husband's sins. "Neglect" for Marv had probably meant he had to microwave his own dinner once a week. The man was priceless.

"He got kind of jealous of the time I spent with Spring." Sarah examined her grimy fingernails. "That was odd, him resenting my absence when I put up with his one-night stands for so long." I heard the anguish in her voice, but she swallowed and went on. "One night when he came home drunk I got really angry and said it had to stop. Marv said he wouldn't drink so much if I stayed home and let our son raise his own kid. I tried to explain to him that James needs a lot of support." Her tone changed. "James would never hurt Spring on purpose. It's just that he's stressed with no job and everything."

I began to understand why Spring was in Petoskey. Sarah had removed her from her father's reach. Though her method was bizarre and she couldn't admit it, Sarah knew the child was both abused and neglected.

"I confronted Marv with everything I've put up with from him all these years. I said something about you and Ben, how you'd been so happy together." Sarah bit her lip. "I was really mad, and I said it wasn't fair that you lost the man who loved you and I had to put up with a man who hurt me, every single day of our marriage."

Sarah's voice sank to a whisper. "That's when Marv told

me he'd been 'consoling' you since Ben died. I was stunned. I didn't know what to say."

"Did you try 'I don't believe for a minute that my best friend would do something like that?' That would have been appropriate." I hardly recognized my own voice, dripping with bitterness.

"As a matter of fact, I did, for a while. But then he told me things—" She stopped, apparently unwilling to recall the nasty details. What had Marv come up with to convince her of the supposed truth of his story: dates and times, locations for our supposed trysts, details of shared passion? It was beyond credibility.

"And after a while you believed him."

"Yes. I said you two could have each other if you were so eager to be together. I'd move in with James and Spring so I could see that she was raised right." She paused, shaking her head. "I had no idea what that would do to him."

As if I were inside his greasy little mind, I saw exactly what Marv had done. He couldn't deny his unfaithfulness, but he'd wanted Sarah to stay. She was comfortable, she was a good wife, and Marv was no doubt aware that he shared, no matter how undeservedly, the glow of propriety she generated in the community. When a new Sarah emerged, one ready to admit he was a lost cause, he'd done what he had to do. Marv had thrown himself on his wife's mercy, groveled for forgiveness, promised to change his ways, and best of all, given her someone else to be mad at.

With the cunning he was known for, Marv Leigh had confused his wife by directing her anger at me. Insensitive as he was, he must have noticed Sarah's growing dissatisfaction at her role as second in command, her longing for an identity of her own. He'd lied to her, and Sarah had been so willing to be lied to that it wasn't even a hard sell.

Pushing personal questions aside I said, "Okay, let's skip Marv and his true confessions for a minute. You say Spring is safe for now, but the caregiver is probably wondering where you are."

"I told the lady I'm Spring's guardian, but I had to have minor surgery. I don't know what she'll do if I'm not there to pick her up on Monday."

I could hardly believe Sarah had accomplished all this. Fueled by spite and desperation, she'd become a different person. It was hard to comprehend, but we had more pressing issues.

"Let's move on to exactly why two guys abducted you and then me. It's something to do with my book, right?"

"You didn't want it," Sarah said defensively. "I rescued it for Spring's sake."

"You *stole* it." It wasn't a time to argue, but I couldn't help it.

"It was ages since you even thought about it. I did some of the research in the beginning, and it was a lot of work to get it published." Her tone was defiant, but she kept her face turned from mine, as if she couldn't sustain the lie directly.

"Something went wrong."

She suddenly leaned forward, as if her stomach hurt. "I couldn't have known."

"Known what?"

"That they'd think I know what they did. It's a lot like what happened in the book."

I recalled that the police had come to question Sarah, thinking she knew something about the real crimes. If the Bay View robberies and the death of the bar owner were related, the thieves had murdered one of their own.

"I put the two incidents together to make an interesting story," I said. "I never dreamed that really happened."

"You made it interesting, all right." Sarcasm from Sarah Leigh! Things were tense indeed. "They think I got the story from a man who's dead now."

"Pete?"

"Yes. In the book one of the robbers tells the woman who cuts his hair that he's going to get a lot of money soon."

"But it's been years since the robberies. Why does anybody care now what happened in the book?"

"Because after this Pete died, they found out he'd moved the stuff. Since the book mentioned a hairdresser, they thought Pete told her—me—where he hid it." Sarah's tone had turned accusing, as if I'd gotten her into trouble. She couldn't have it both ways, insisting on one hand the book was her work and on the other hand being mad at me for writing it.

I forced my thoughts back to the more critical question of why we were creep-quarry at this point. "Why would this Pete tell you where he hid stolen goods?"

"He didn't. I never met the man."

"I know that. Why do his buddies think he did?"

"Recently they learned about some cabin over here that he stayed in sometimes."

I knew where that came from. My chat with Angie had reminded her of the summer her brother spent in Abaletta.

"They looked everywhere else, Russ said. Because, uh, the book's author lives in Abaletta, they think Pete hid the stuff here, in or near that cabin. They're looking for someone who can tell them."

"Too bad they got stupid and killed old Pete."

"I think that was Russ. The other guy, Zane, doesn't talk much, but he seems a little more human."

I filed that information away. "I still don't see why they think you know where Pete stashed the stuff. In the book, it's the detective who figures it out, not the hairdresser."

Sarah's voice became a whisper. "James sort of hinted I knew details about the robberies that wasn't in the book."

"James knows these guys?"

"No, he doesn't know them!" Sarah's response was petulant. "After the book came out, this policeman called and wanted to talk to me about his old case."

"Detective Oskar. I've met him."

"I told him I was really busy and he should call back."

"Because you didn't want to answer his questions."

Ignoring me, Sarah went on. "While I was out one day he called again, and James was at my house, doing his laundry. Oskar told James they were interested in how I knew the robberies and the murder were related. They wondered if I might have spoken to Pete at some point."

I saw it coming. James, who had never been important enough in his own estimation, was pitifully eager to impress others when an opportunity arose. "James told Oskar you knew more than you included in the book."

As usual, Sarah had an alibi for her son. "James said I'd acted funny about the whole thing. He thought I felt guilty because I'd withheld information from the police."

"When you actually felt guilty about stealing my work."

"Not guilty, just a little nervous."

I sat back, putting it all together. Since Sarah was the supposed author of the book and she was a hairdresser, Russ thought Pete had told her about his hiding place, however unlikely that was.

"Did you tell them the story is fiction?"

Sarah grimaced. "Russ doesn't believe me."

That was understandable. Being a liar himself, Russ naturally distrusted everyone else. I sighed. "How did they manage to abduct you?"

For a while I thought there would be no answer as Sarah stared into one leaf-cluttered corner of the shack. Finally she spoke, haltingly, as if pushing the words out by force.

"I went out to the lake, and—I was doing something…"

"Faking your death and setting me up as the murderer." My tone was harsher than I'd intended. Though I wanted to maintain calm, my words came out in a rush. "You snatched my sweater to leave in the van. You wrote a note saying you were afraid of me and mailed it to Tom Finch. At the lake you staged what looked like a struggle and a body being disposed of. All that was arranged to implicate me after our fight at the school, and you almost pulled it off."

Sarah stared ahead, her chin trembling. "I've been asking James to let us adopt Spring, but he says no."

Of course he would say that. Spring was James' guarantee that his mother would never give up on him.

"I tried to get Marv to help me convince James. He knows she'd be better off with us, but he says we're too old to take on a child that young. A few months ago I started thinking of ways for Spring and me to disappear, just the two of us. It wasn't any I ever meant to act on, but things kept getting worse. Marv was good for a while after…that night, but he's staying out again, and he's drinking more than ever."

"I'm sorry, Sarah."

Swallowing, she went on. "James is so far in debt he's going to go under, and he isn't a good father to Spring. I asked him again last week to at least come back home so Spring can live with us, but James can be stubborn sometimes."

Wonder where that came from.

Even if Sarah convinced James to give her custody, he'd always be around, sponging off his parents and influencing the child. What chance did Spring have in life with a violent father and a drunken grandfather?

Sarah's face was blank as she said the words I'd been waiting to hear. "The book was there, right in front of me. I knew it was good, so I took it. You didn't need the money, but Spring and I needed a new start. I cashed the advance check and put it in a box under my bed. In my dreams Spring and I would disappear someday, and no one would ever find us."

It was just as Rachel had speculated. By sheer determination, Sarah had convinced herself of the rightness of her actions. It had all been for Spring's benefit, and everyone else, even a life-long friend, took second place.

"I guess Russ and Zane followed me out to the lake, and bad things started happening from there." Sarah spoke as if everything she'd done was justified, and only the interference of two criminals had caused all the trouble we were in.

Chapter Twenty-two

As we huddled in the shack, our wet clothes clinging and our stressed muscles aching, Sarah told me her harebrained, wildly hopeful scheme. "The lake was a perfect place to disappear. With all the stuff down there, failure to recover the bodies wouldn't be surprising. In my original plan it was an accident, so I was waiting for summer." She smiled shyly. "I don't even know if I really meant to do it. It was just something to think about."

"Then you began to realize you couldn't pull off being an author."

Her nod was both affirmation and surrender. "After James told the detective I knew more than I did, I felt like I was drowning in lies. My fantasy turned into a necessity.

"Blaming you wasn't part of the original plan, but when I heard at the school you're publishing a book, everything got worse. Between questions from the police and your interference, it would all come out. Everyone would know you're the writer, not me, and I'd be nobody again."

So much irony, I thought. While I'd spent years feeling inferior to Sarah because of her innate goodness, she'd seen herself as unimportant. It was true in some ways: Sarah didn't come first for her children and certainly not for her husband. Even those who praised her good works thought of Sarah as supporting causes, not leading them.

I felt very small to have let things get so bad between us. Sarah had been there for me when my life fell apart. Yet when her crises arose—facing the truth about Marv and learning the depth of James' ugliness—I'd been busy pretending I didn't care that our friendship had died.

Confused by Sarah's coldness, I had pulled away, and she'd lost her last connection to the person who understood her best. Rachel was right. I should have asked Sarah point blank what was wrong. Instead I'd retired into my shell of hurt, and Sarah's feelings had intensified. My small-town successes must have seemed to her the height of achievement. What had she wanted from life other than a loving husband, two normal kids, and the chance to do things her fellow citizens found admirable?

In the end she'd taken a drastic step to extricate herself from the life she didn't want anymore, and just when it seemed to be working, she'd faced unanswerable questions about the authorship of the book.

Sarah stared at the rough plank wall like a sleepwalker. "When you asked me to go with you to Shoepac, things I'd pictured for months became possible. The solution to all my problems was right there. If I did what I'd been thinking about, the questions would end, and Spring would be safe with me."

"You'd let James think his child is dead?"

Sarah set her lips. "James has decided he's not Spring's father. It doesn't matter to me, even if it's true." Sarah dealt with her son in a final comment. "He's the beneficiary of my life insurance. He'll have to figure out the rest on his own."

I lowered my eyes to avoid the pain in hers. "So instead of waiting for summer, you had to disappear right away. An accident wasn't going to work, since there was no reason for you and Spring to be out in a canoe at this time of year."

"Yes. It had to be murder." Sarah was matter-of-fact. I took her to a day care place in Petoskey I found on the Internet and began making the arrangements."

"To point the blame at me."

She sighed. "To make you pay for what you did."

"Which is nothing."

Sarah's brow arched. "So you say."

I bit my lip to keep from answering, and she continued. "I went home, wrote the note, mailed it, then went to the lake and made it look like Spring and I had been drowned."

"By me." It was overkill, but I didn't care.

She waved a hand. "They'd never have brought charges. I've seen the way Damon Bates looks at you." Her expression hardened. "I just wanted you to suffer a little."

I couldn't even be angry at something so pitiful. "Sarah, there's nothing between Marv and me. If you'd stop being mad, your head knows that."

"He told me!" she argued stubbornly. "You said I'd never guess because I'm too trusting and a little bit dumb. You said you always have to lead because I can't do anything by myself."

I gave up. "Let's not play 'Did Too, Did Not', okay? Just tell me what really happened at the lake."

"When I dumped the spare tire and got back to shore, those two were waiting for me. They asked where their stuff was, but I had no idea what they were talking about. Russ put me in the back seat of their pickup while Zane brushed away their tracks. Russ said—" She stopped as tears choked her voice. "He said they'd hurt Spring if I didn't tell them what I learned from Pete."

"It's okay," I soothed, afraid she'd go into hysterics now

the threat was over—sort of. "Do they know where she is?"

Sarah sat up straight, shaking her head. "No one does."

"But they didn't believe that you never met Pete?"

"At first Russ thought I'd found the stolen stuff, and that's why I was planning to disappear. I told him that wasn't true. I think he believed me about that part, but he still thought I knew where that guy Pete hid the loot."

The word *loot* sounded funny coming from Sarah, who's no gangster or gangsta or any other tough type. According to Detective Oskar, Russ Ranett didn't care who got hurt in his schemes, and that fit with what I'd seen. I hoped we'd have no opportunity to get to know Mr. Ranett any better.

"So what happened then?"

"They took me to that hunting cabin. I was blindfolded, but I knew we were near the landfill, because I could hear the beeps as the garbage trucks backed up. We stayed there for what seemed like a week while they tried to find out where the cabin Pete stayed in is. They kept asking me about places on the map. I did my best to help, but I told them there were things in the book I didn't create—"

"Like all of it."

She ignored me. "They wanted to know who else might

have talked to Pete."

"And you gave them my name."

"I did not!" Sarah was indignant. "I said a friend had helped with the book, but she never met Pete either. Russ said he'd do some checking. He came back very smug and told Zane they needed to find Caroline Batzer."

"So they would have come for me anyway."

"They left me alone when they went to grab you. They didn't think I could squeeze out that window, but I did."

"Hence the scrape on your arm. But you called Marv earlier."

Sarah nodded. "They both went outside and left me alone for a few minutes. The phone rang and rang, and when he finally answered I could tell he was in bad shape. Then I heard Russ coming and had to hang up. He was suspicious, so I was afraid to use the phone again until they both left."

"And then you pulled me into your troubles."

She raised her hands as if asking what else she could have done. "I called Marv first. He didn't answer, so I called you."

"Why me?"

She looked confused, as if she didn't know either. "I guess I'm just used to you being there when I need you.

Suddenly it was like...the other...never happened."

"It didn't, Sarah." I left it at that, and so did she.

"The window was really small," she said, as if the details of her escape were important right now. "I had to throw my pants out first and wriggle through in my underwear."

I wondered what she'd have done if she'd been unable to get through and been left inside the cabin without pants. I felt a tiny smile at the picture but sobered at the thought my hips would never have fit through that skimpy opening.

Instead of phoning the sheriff for help, Sarah had dragged me into her disaster. Again I had to resist the urge to smack her. Sarah watched the empty road, oblivious.

"The landfill staff should get here soon."

I looked at my watch. "Yeah, it's almost nine. Why did you wait for me at the cabin? Why didn't you start walking?"

"I was afraid I'd meet them coming back. If I went through the woods, I'd have missed you. I figured we'd be gone before they returned."

"But they weren't away for long, since I wasn't at home."

How had they learned my name in the first place? From the police? From someone else?

No, it had been my own doing. I'd called Angie's number

and given my name. That had been a mistake.

Still, playing knight—make that lady—in shining armor to Sarah meant that I'd walked right into their clutches. Maybe I deserved to have my novel stolen, because I sure hadn't seen this plot line developing.

"Someone's coming!" Sarah exclaimed. "Here, we're over here!" Before I could react, she jumped up and ran out of the lean-to. A gray pickup had turned off the gravel road and into the landfill drive. It contained two men, and though I couldn't see them clearly, my brain went on alert. I remembered what I should have known all along.

"Sarah, it's Sunday!" I called. "The landfill's closed!"

She froze, and the truck skidded to a stop. Our only good luck was that the gate was closed. Our two least favorite people couldn't come after us with the vehicle, but they left it quickly, their intentions evident.

"Run!" I shouted, doing as I commanded at the same time. I headed for the trees, but Sarah just stood there. It wasn't until a gunshot rang out that she came to life, scampering after me like Atalanta herself.

We ran, arms pumping and lungs puffing like the forty-somethings we were. I hate to admit it, but it was me this time who caused our downfall. I looked back to see if Sarah had made the tree line and ran smack into a branch at forehead level. That's all I knew for some time.

Chapter Twenty-three

I awoke to discomfort. My arms and legs wouldn't move, and my neck felt like jolts of electrical current were coursing through it. My head didn't feel too good either. I opened one eye a little, gauging how much that was going to hurt. In the slit appeared Sarah, sitting opposite me and duct-taped, as I was, to a chair. She heaved a sigh of relief when I showed signs of life. Misery loves company.

We were back at the cabin. On the wavy loveseat Russ sprawled, snoring, while Zane sat at the table playing a video game on his phone. He must have sensed my change of state, because he looked over at me then rose to poke Russ awake. The smile appeared almost at once, and I wondered how he could wake up in that kind of mood. Then again, he had what he wanted—us.

"So how you doin'?" he asked, sitting up and rubbing his stubbly chin with a grubby-looking hand.

"I'll live." My voice sounded crackly.

Russ chuckled as if I'd said something funny, and I realized it was a bad choice of words in light of our very short future. "Let's start over. You wrote that book, which means you're the one that met Pete somehow, somewhere."

I looked to Sarah, whose eyes tried to tell me something. It took a few seconds and determined dismissal of the pain in my head, but I figured it out. She'd kept us alive by admitting I'd written the book. She'd probably explained that I was the one who could lead them to what they were after. That was true, sort of. I'd remembered where the cabin was, though I doubted it would keep us alive for long.

I tried honesty one more time. "Listen to me. I made it up. I heard on the news about the robberies, and then later there was the story of the guy found...in the woods." My still-throbbing brain censored use of the word *murdered.* "I thought it would be clever to put them into a story together."

"You're lying," Russ said without rancor. "Why'd you call Angie if you didn't have something to offer us?"

Shaking my head I asked, "If I knew where some stolen goods are hidden, why didn't I go get them myself?"

"You haven't got the nerve, maybe. Or you don't know how to make money off of it." He leaned forward, into my personal space. "Now tell me where it is, or we'll get nasty."

I thought they already had.

The image of the cabin with the Red Man sign had floated through my mind until I recalled its location. "I can't tell you where it is. I'll have to show you."

Russ' smile got bigger. "See, Zane? I told you they knew."

"I haven't actually been there," I said, "but Pete told me about it."

Sarah looked surprised, and I shot her a warning glance. These men were going to kill us, and all I could do was make them think they needed us for a bit longer. They thought I'd met Pete, so I'd claim that I had. My storytelling skills would have to be at their best, though, or we were two fried not-so-green tomatoes.

Russ settled back on the loveseat, and a little cloud of musty dust rose around him. His gaze stayed locked on mine, and I got the same sensation I once had when I stepped on something cold and found a mouse's head my cat had left on the floor: first a chill, then dread, then an ominous feeling there was worse to come.

"I was working," I told them. "Pete came into the emergency room with a strained shoulder. He'd been drinking, and while he waited for X-rays, I asked how he hurt himself. He said he'd moved some heavy stuff to a safe place."

"A safe place! You hear that, Zane?"

Zane didn't answer. Russ turned back to me, gesturing for me to go on. "He said he had trouble getting it out of the boat," I went on. "That's how his shoulder got strained."

213

"A boat. Did you hear that, Zane? He used a boat!"

Zane frowned slightly, as if irritated by Russ' frequent interruptions.

"Just making conversation, I said I liked canoeing the lakes around here. Pete said I probably hadn't seen the place he'd been at because it was on a lake that's really swampy. Then he said something like it was just a shack but it was worth a bundle now." I paused, hoping I hadn't gone too far. Zane and Russ were both listening intently. I finished, "Then he said something about a tobacco cabin. I don't remember exactly how he put it, and it didn't make sense to me at the time. As I said, he was pretty intoxicated. They couldn't even give him painkillers for the shoulder until he sobered up."

"Sounds just like old Pete."

From the frequent accidents Angie had mentioned, I'd deduced her brother might have been a drinker, and my guess paid off. They were buying the story, so I finished it off. "When I wrote my book, I used the idea of a guy hiding stolen goods on his buddies, but as I said earlier, it was just a story. It wasn't until Angie told me about her brother and described the Red Man sign on the cabin that I put it all together."

Now that I'd given them reason to keep us alive a while longer, I asked a question. "I read the reports of Pete's supposedly accidental death not long afterward. What really happened?"

"I think you can guess," Russ replied. "He had the stuff we got from the places in Bay View, and he was supposed to keep it safe until the cops stopped watching me and we could find buyers for it. Pete couldn't hold his liquor, though, and I heard he was blabbing all over about how he had big money coming in. We decided—" A small move from Zane, no more than a shifting of those huge laterals, made Russ rephrase. "—I decided to end our association."

"You shot him."

Russ glanced at Zane, whose expression turned more glum than usual. "You'd have to hear the whole story to understand, but that was the result."

I pictured a drive in Russ' car and a confrontation over Pete's refusal to turn over the goods. Russ must have thought he knew where the stash was, but Pete had been both smarter and dumber than he should have been: smart to hide the loot well, but dumb to go anywhere alone with Russ.

"We looked everywhere, and we found nothing all this time. Then you came along and reminded Angie about the cabin. We finally got lucky, right Zane?"

Zane simply moved his ebony eyes from me to Russ then

back again, waiting.

"You think Pete took a boatload of stolen stuff to that cabin."

"Yup. We had some paintings, at least a dozen. And there's some jewelry that's pretty nice in a box about this big." Russ' hands shaped an eight-by-sixteen inch rectangle.

"There's silver," Zane put in.

"Oh, yeah. We had a setting for sixteen in silver." Russ made it sound like it had been in his family for generations. Though his next statement was casual, I sensed he'd reached the important part. "The biggest piece was an African figurine in wood about the size of a twelve-pack. It's mahogany that's carved on all four sides."

The newspaper article I'd read came back to me. A senile man had hidden a diamond necklace inside a curiosity piece and forgotten to tell his heirs. Russ and his cronies stole the African sculpture, and now they knew there was something even more valuable inside it. No wonder there was renewed interest in finding Pete's cache.

I didn't let on that I knew the importance of the piece. "All the stuff would fit in a large trunk or crate."

"Most likely."

"And he probably put it inside, where it would stay dry."

"Right. We just need to know where the Red Man cabin is at."

"It's a small lake way on the other side of town."

Russ slapped his knees and rose. "Let's go take a look."

"The only way to get to it this time of year is by canoe."

He thought about that. "You've been there though, right? And you can handle a canoe."

"I've never been to the cabin itself. I don't trespass."

"Well, you're going to now. Zane, let's get this woman ready to travel."

I noted the reference to me alone and felt a stab of fear. Sarah was no longer needed. One more death wouldn't bother Russ according to my gauge of his character—or lack of it. Desperately I looked around the room for an escape route, an idea, anything. Russ rose and stretched like an arrogant cat, but two pairs of eyes were on me. Sarah's desperate face showed her understanding that she wouldn't be going along. Zane's stoic gaze took in my distress and reflected nothing. Still, he spoke in a voice as flat as his eyes.

"We'll take them both."

Russ stopped abruptly, dropping his arms. "Why?"

Indicating Sarah, he said, "This one makes the other one behave."

Russ took that in, looking from Sarah to me carefully. I tried to look just anxious enough. "Okay," he said with a shrug. "We've got the back seat."

If you've ever had to actually ride in the back seat of a pickup truck, I hope you're younger than I am. They might be fine for small children and extra teenaged girlfriends, but for two middle-aged women still suffering from a night in the woods and hours tied to wooden chairs, it was the next step in torture. We crouched in our tiny space, unable to see much over the tall seats in front of us. I was miserable, and Sarah looked almost comatose.

We bumped along the gravel road then smoothed out a bit as we made the highway. I directed from the back, craning my neck to see where we were and giving the next instruction to Zane, who drove carefully, watching his speed and signaling turns well in advance. No traffic stops.

Russ made us duck even farther down as we passed through Abaletta, and I almost sobbed as the tops of familiar buildings passed. *If Sally looked out her window right now, she might wonder who the two strange men in town were,* I thought, and as we passed the used car lot, *Jim Fletcher's in there. He'd help us.* Irrelevantly I recalled a story he'd told about calling his wife a few months back.

"Shouldn't you be at a library meeting?" he'd asked her.

"Oh my gosh, I forgot to write it down." she answered. "How did you know?"

"I was sitting out in front of the store and first Marilyn Schnepp drove by, then Pat Osbourne, then Alice Green. When Barb Huffman went past I knew there had to be a library meeting. The only one on the committee who didn't go by was you."

It was one of those small-town stories that demonstrate how wrapped up we are in each other's lives. Of course, nothing was notable about another dusty pickup passing through town. Before we knew it, we'd turned onto Highway 28 and Abaletta was in the rearview mirror. It had never been dearer to me than at that moment, and I saw Sarah wipe away a tear when she thought I didn't see.

A few miles out of town we passed a party store that rented canoes and rowboats. This brought about a complicated maneuver to prevent Sarah and me from calling attention to ourselves. Zane drove down a side road until we were out of sight, and Russ ordered us out. We stood on the roadside in the chilly air, the sun barely a presence behind the clouds that had reappeared as the day progressed.

Zane left, heading to the store to rent two canoes and buy groceries. I was getting somewhat used to the presence of the gun Russ held so casually. I considered taking off, but it wasn't much of an idea. I'd have to cross a large open space before I reached any sort of cover, and what about Sarah? Russ might shoot her from pure irritation.

We began to shiver as the wait grew long. The air temperature wasn't bad, but the wind was sharp, chasing the clouds above past at a rapid pace. There were still damp places in my clothes, and I wished the sun would come out and bake them dry.

To distract myself I pictured the scene at the party store, Zane renting two canoes from the proprietor, Edna Schlak. I could almost feel sorry for the man. A person has to know Edna well to be able to read her. Kindness is a screechy, "What do you want?" and an eagle-eyed glare as she leans across her ancient wooden countertop. The fact that she's scrawny, homely, and has an honest-to-goodness glass eye is enough like a scene from a slasher movie to scare anyone with bad nerves. Zane might not understand that as long as she wasn't chasing him out of the store with a broom, Edna was being perfectly civil. For Edna.

When Zane returned he said nothing, but I'd gotten used to that. He brought the supplies Russ had ordered, and two canoes now protruded from the truck's bed. Climbing back in, we took off. With little else to do for the next ten miles, I studied Sarah Mathews Leigh, wondering how we'd come to this.

What I concluded was that childhood closeness often comes from simple proximity. In a small town, there aren't a lot of friendship choices to make. We'd lived three blocks apart, attended the same school and church. In all likelihood we'd stuck together out of inertia more than anything else. We'd done things together because we did the same things.

Now that I wasn't puzzling out the whys of Sarah's rejection, I began to look at our separation differently. Whatever its cause, we'd both grown from it. Maybe Sarah had subconsciously recognized the need to break the bond between us so we could truly become individuals. Don't they say that later in life, after she's fulfilled her obligations to family, work, and community, a woman can become what she's always wanted to be? I wanted to be an author. Sarah evidently wanted to be two things: Spring's guardian and a person recognized as important in her own right.

Though the way she'd treated me still stung, I had to

admit I was stronger because of it. To avoid Sarah's frowns, I'd branched into new directions and made new choices. Looking past how dumb my method was, the fact remained it was what I wanted, and I might never have taken the plunge if it hadn't been for the situation. Many things I liked about my life lately wouldn't have happened if Sarah and I had gone on the way we always had.

Had Sarah done any of this out of concern for me? Of course not, but we'd both been successful in a way. Without me to lean on, she'd made herself a person of her own. If her opinions were no longer mine, that wasn't all bad. Stealing the book was wrong, but I recognized both her concern for her grandchild and the fear her identity was so wrapped up with mine that she had none.

The strangest part of all was that we now had to depend on each other as never before. Having grown apart, we were forced together in a new way, and our cooperation was the only hope we had of living through this ordeal. Sarah suddenly raised her eyes to mine, and I saw, as I'd always been able to see, that she had read what I was thinking, as she had always been able to do.

Chapter Twenty-four

The Double Lakes are more like four or five lakes, but they meld into each other and separate depending on the time of year and the amount of rain we've had. They aren't populated, because they lie on land owned by a paper mill and because the swampy shores already mentioned aren't much good for recreation. They are pretty, though, and Ben and I had braved the mucky banks to canoe them a few times over the years.

Following my directions, Zane pulled off the gravel road onto an even less traveled two-track. That took us to a fork, where I told him to keep to the right though the left path was better traveled. A small wooden sign, almost obscured by last year's woody weed stalks, indicated there was a boat ramp to the right. From the looks of the road, nobody cared.

We bumped along, barely able to see the faint track that led into a grove of skinny, densely-packed poplar and birch trees. The ground rose and fell, with washouts so deep a car would never have made it through. At one point water covered the road, and a mother duck led six babies across, sailing in a determined line and ignoring our rude interruption of their passage.

Once we'd cleared that hurdle the road turned sharply, and we came to the lake. It was shallow until the middle, where a deep spot offered local fishermen bass, perch, and a few pike. The shore was ragged, with too many little inlets to count. In bygone summers, Ben and I had spied on turtles sunning themselves on protruding logs, laughing at the multiple "plunks" as they slid into the water at our approach. In a few months lilies would float gracefully along the surface, but now the water was greenly cold and the shoreline barren.

Across the lake and around a bend was the cabin. I assured the doubting Russ he'd see it once we were afloat. As Zane busied himself unloading the canoes and carrying them to the water's edge, I wondered what went on in the man's head. Was he in favor of killing two women in cold blood? That was surely what Russ had in mind once he had what he wanted. If they weighted our bodies and sank them in the marshy lake, no one would ever know what became of us.

The canoe trip was unlike any I'd ever known. The frigid water cooled the metal skin of the canoe to a painful chill. Since I was the only one with any experience, I assumed the crossing wouldn't be quick, but Zane was a natural athlete. He took to paddling after only a few strokes, pushing the canoe forward with confident strokes. It was good that he and Sarah shared a craft, because she huddled in the front, holding the sides like a cat avoiding a bath. Michigan lakes don't warm until summer (if then), and it wouldn't take long to succumb to the shocking chill if a canoe went over.

My problem was Russ, who'd made a few muttered comments along the way about distrusting canoes but didn't reveal until time to board that he was actually terrified of them. Though they feel tippy, canoes aren't as bad as they seem. There is a trick to staying upright, however, and flailing isn't involved. Russ peered over one side then the other as I paddled, making my job more difficult. Finally I barked, "Sit up and sit still!" Surprisingly, he obeyed with no argument, but for once the desire to grin had deserted him.

The lake was silent. On the water every sound carries, but all we heard was the quiet slurp of the paddles' draw as they lifted and fell. Zane let me take the lead, copying my movements until he achieved maximum efficiency. It's not rocket science, but paddling correctly saves wear and tear on a person's upper-body muscles. With shoulders like Zane's, no worries.

Muscles I hadn't used in years let me know I'd taken on an overly strenuous task. Part of the pain was due to pride.

Zane's strong arms pushed the paddle easily through the water, and I was unwilling to fall behind or appear to be struggling. Russ noticed nothing, but Sarah watched our silent competition miserably from her slouch. Hurrying to my death. What irony!

The cabin appeared once we made a turn into an irregularly shaped nook. Seeing the Red Man sign, I breathed a small sigh of relief. I had remembered the correct location.

By the time we landed I was trembling with fatigue. I tried not to look pained as I unbent my legs and back and waded to shore. Russ was anxious to exit the canoe, but he waited until I pulled it almost completely out of the water. Once his feet were on dry land, his grin reappeared, along with the gun. We waited as Zane dragged the canoes into the brush and kicked the wet sand around to hide the marks they'd made. I thought that overly cautious. This time of year, there was no one around for miles.

The cabin before us was different from and yet depressingly like the cabin we'd left earlier. Neither was a place I'd have chosen for my last day on earth. This one was larger than the other, and was what they call *vintage*, meaning old but not yet antique. It was probably built in the late '40s, since it had tan shingles for siding, the kind that are supposed to look like bricks. Maybe they do from far enough away. The roof had regular black shingles with moss growing on them, not a good sign. The front door's frame sat a foot above the sand as the ground slanted down to the lakeshore. It looked pretty solid, and Russ made only one attempt to batter it open before seeking another means of entry. At his order, we followed him around the structure.

There were windows, but they were shuttered and high enough off the ground to make forcing them difficult. Leaving them as a possibility if later efforts failed, we continued to the back, where we found an enclosed porch with a battered screen/storm door. While Russ looked around for something with which to break the glass, I reached forward and tried the knob, which opened with an antique squawk.

The area we stepped into was about six by six. To one side was a rack for storing wood. A few good-sized pieces remained along the bottom, their bark littering the concrete floor. Another door blocked our way, this one locked. Russ looked at me. "Now what, Miz Smart-Ass?"

I looked around at the walls of the entry, since people who have cabins often leave a spare key hidden somewhere. It's no fun to travel for hours and discover on arrival that the means to get inside is home in a desk drawer. In only a few seconds I found an honest-to-goodness skeleton key, wrapped in oilcloth and hung with a leather thong to a nail behind the wood rack. Russ unlocked the door and showed his sickening grin as he ushered us inside.

The cabin was three rooms: a large square served as common area composed of kitchen, dining, and living space. A fireplace in one wall was black with soot, and a good-sized crack ran up its side, not boding well for utility. Two doors on the left wall stood open, revealing bedrooms. One was equipped with two bunks, the other with four, room for a real snore-fest when filled with fishermen. There was no bathroom, but I'd guessed that, having noted an outhouse as we skirted the building. It hadn't looked inviting, but then, I've never seen an outhouse that did.

No stash of treasure jumped out at us, and Russ was immediately resentful. "If we did all this for nothing, lady—" His smile turned threatening.

"Pete would have put it somewhere out of sight, wouldn't he?" Sarah asked, and I shot her a grateful look.

"I suppose," Russ allowed. "It's too late now to do much looking though."

He was right. It was March, and our days still ended

early. Despite the fact Zane had bought some large flashlights at the canoe rental, it would be difficult to search unfamiliar territory in failing light. Wordlessly, Zane went to the front door, unlocked it, and disappeared, returning in a few seconds with an armload of supplies. I hoped he'd bought plenty of food. I couldn't remember the last time I'd eaten.

As Zane left for a second load, Russ couldn't resist looking around. Moving through the cabin with a flashlight, he looked under anything remotely large enough to conceal something else. In the smaller bedroom he found something.

"You. Come and help me move this," he ordered. I took one side of a chest of drawers, one of those particle-board things that weigh a ton and leave your hands full of slivers. Behind it, a piece of paneling about two feet by four was nailed to the wall. Russ spoke as if I'd be as glad as he at the discovery. "See if you can pry it off on that side."

I looked around the place for a pry-bar. Over the door someone had hung some sort of logging tool, a metal hook that had once had a long handle. Taking it down, I stuck the hook in sideways, sliding it behind the wooden cover. Seeing my intent, Russ took over, pulling at it until the nails screamed and pulled loose from the wall. He did the same on the other side, and we both pulled at the board until it came free. I found myself almost as interested as he at the prospect of discovering hidden treasure, even if would never be mine.

Behind the panel was the back side of the Red Man sign. Long ago, someone had patched a hole, possibly an old chimney, with what they had lying around. Throwing the hook to the floor with a clank, Russ swore in disgust.

Zane appeared in the door behind us, taking in the situation. "Where's the other one?"

It took us both a second to get his meaning, and Russ understood sooner than I did. His curse this time was longer, more fervent, and much less socially acceptable. It was a good thing—maybe the only good thing at that moment—that prissy old Sarah Leigh wasn't there to hear it.

Zane moved quickly out the back door. Russ started to follow but returned to grab my arm and jerk me along, determined not to lose his other captive.

Sarah was gone. Behind the cabin the ground was covered with old pine needles, soft underfoot and unlikely to yield prints. While Russ ranted, Zane, a man of action, searched the area in ever-widening arcs, looking for any sign of her passing. His expression didn't reflect much hope.

Dragging me back into the cabin, Russ spent the next hour "personalizing" the smaller bedroom, which had a window with the heavy shutters typical of older cottages. This he closed off by wedging some bed slats across the louvers. Using a rock, he replaced the paneling that covered the hole and then pulled the dresser into place in front of it.

While he worked, Russ ordered me to make us all something to eat. "And make noise," he snarled. "If I don't hear you, I'm coming out there."

Since I was half-starved, I hardly noticed things that would have driven me nuts at home. Signs of mice were everywhere, though I saw no dark forms scurrying in any of the room's corners. There was a pump in the kitchen that only coughed air when I tried it, which meant no clean water for washing. A sad-looking bar of Ivory soap was almost gone, gnawed by hungry critters to a mere nub. I had no way to warm the food, since Russ refused to let me build a fire for fear someone would see the smoke.

As I prepared our dinner, my mind worked overtime. Sarah's escape might increase my chances of survival, but I feared otherwise. It was a long walk out of here, through swampy terrain, and Zane was combing the woods for her. If she did evade him and make it out, alerting the authorities would endanger everything she'd done thus far. If she stuck to her original idea and disappeared, Sarah had everything to gain and nothing to lose. In addition to all that, sending help would benefit the person she least wanted to assist.

I prepared cold beans and cold hot dogs (a sad oxymoron), Pepsi at room temperature, and marshmallows. When I pulled them from the grocery bag, Zane's stony face came to mind. Did the silent giant have an inner child who wanted to imagine this was a camping trip? I shrugged and popped one into my mouth. Sugar equals energy, which I'd need if I got the chance to run again.

Zane returned gloomier than ever, having seen no sign of Sarah. "We should go."

Russ looked up from where he crouched, searching under a bunk. "Why?"

"She'll tell the police where we are."

Russ smiled patronizingly. "What was she doing when we found her, Zane? Trying to disappear. Now she has a second chance. To everybody but us she's dead already." He made a curl in the air with a hand then leveled it out like a disappearing trail. "Miz Leigh's going to head for the hills."

My very thought, but I refused to let Russ have the last word. "You wouldn't know about friendship and loyalty."

Russ smirked. "From what I understand about this book

thing, I don't think Miz Leigh does either. If she makes it out of here, she faces arrest for everything from plagiarism to kidnapping. She'll head for the nearest bus station."

Zane wasn't impressed. "What if she doesn't?"

"She still has to walk out of here. It's dark, it's swampy, and it's the boonies. She won't reach a road until noon tomorrow at the earliest. So we get up early, find the stuff, and get out before she can send anybody."

I agreed with Russ. Sarah probably didn't want to help me, and if she did, she'd be too late. My assessment of her chances was even lower than Russ', knowing as I did what a terrible sense of direction she had.

Zane didn't seem as certain as Russ was, but he didn't argue. Clearly Russ was the brains of the outfit.

We ate our pitiful meal hungrily, all of us having used up a good share of our reserves during the past twenty-four hours. After I gathered up the paper plates and cups we'd used and stowed them in a plastic bag, Russ commanded, "Time to turn in, lady. We'll get an early start tomorrow."

As soon as I heard snores from the next room, I tried the window. Russ deserved a gold star for improvisation. The shutter opened only half an inch. Likewise, the door to my room was secured on the other side with the ancient chair-under-the-handle technique. No wonder it's used all the time in old movies. The darned thing works.

The dilapidated dresser had a bad leg, a drawer that didn't quite close, and a hunk of veneer missing from its top. As my flashlight beam passed over it, I jumped in surprise. Behind the dresser stood a madwoman, her hair full of leaves and debris. Her face was dotted with scabs, some of which trailed blood, and her eyes were wild and desperate. Realizing it was a mirror, I muttered, "Who put that there? We're camping, for pity's sake."

Laying a musty-smelling blanket out on the skimpy plank bed, I unrolled the sleeping bag Russ had tossed to me. I crawled inside, repelled by its damp coolness until my body heat did its work. My legs ached from running, my arms from paddling, my head from being clobbered by the tree branch. The mattress consisted of hills and valleys of ancient, clumpy cotton, but the discomfort hardly registered. I figured I'd let my body rest while my mind worked out a plan for escape.

That was my last thought of the day. The next thing I knew it was morning, and the rising sun sliced through the louvers, making skinny stripes like the bars of a jail cell on the cabin floor.

Chapter Twenty-five

It was cold. The sleeping bag kept my body fairly comfortable, but the tip of my nose was freezing. I pulled my head in like a turtle, trying to warm it, but that meant breathing in musty odors from old fabric, dust, and, admittedly, me. For a while I lay quietly, waiting for sounds of movement in the next room.

I needed a bathroom, or at the very least an outhouse. Lying perfectly still, I tried to think of something else and ignore the urge. No sense waking those guys up.

A shadow passed across the window, and I rose to peek between the slats, dragging the sleeping bag along as a wrap. Through the grimy, sand-pitted glass I saw Russ, not four feet from me. His stance and expression left no doubt he'd awoken for the same reason I had and was doing something about it. I hurriedly backed away, but when he reentered the cabin, I called out, "Hey! I need to use the facilities."

The chair slid away with a rasp, and the door opened. With a mocking bow, Russ ushered me into the main room where Zane sat at the kitchen table, a breakfast soda in front of him. He'd been as quiet in his rising as he was about everything else.

Gesturing at the back door, Russ said with his usual grin, "Zane will escort you to the privy. Wouldn't want to lose your company."

Zane followed me outside, stopping a polite distance from the outhouse. I looked at it doubtfully. The roof was caved in on one side, the boards rotted away, and the door was missing half a plank. Inside, the bench looked sturdy enough, and a thoughtful builder had provided hinged lids to cover the holes. It was a two-seater, which I've never been able to fathom. Why call it a privy if you have to share it?

With a sigh of resignation I entered and shut the door, using my foot to push it into place. There were spider webs everywhere, but I didn't see any live specimens at present. Using one of the paper napkins I'd grabbed, I chose a lid and lifted. It was stuck. Great. The lid on the right was in working order, and I wiped away the grime of years as best I could. The long period of disuse at least meant the place didn't smell, so it wasn't as bad an experience as some I've had. Before leaving I made a quick check for anything that might be useful against Russ and Zane, but what could an outhouse provide beyond the obvious?

When I emerged, Zane was staring out over the lake, his brow furrowed in an effort to see through the mist on the water. Following his gaze, I tried to make out what he saw. He pointed, and I leaned toward him to sight down his arm at the precise spot. Something broke the surface, actually two things. One was large and grayish and might have been a rock. The other, smaller and white, looked totally out of place in the dark water.

Before I realized what he intended, Zane moved down the beach and into the trees. Crashing into the brush where he'd stashed the canoes the night before, he searched hastily. I couldn't see the canoes, but I guessed from his body language what he'd discovered. One of them wasn't there; it was capsized in the middle of the lake. With a sickening lurch in my stomach, I realized what the floating white thing must be: the oh-so-white cotton jacket Sarah had been wearing.

Zane shouted for Russ, who sauntered out of the cabin. After squinting at the spot, he turned to Zane and shrugged. "I told you she was nothing to worry about."

That was it, Sarah's epitaph as far as he was concerned. One less woman to murder. Zane pulled the second canoe from its hiding place and shoved off, returning in a few minutes with the other canoe in tow.

"Nothing but this," he said, taking the shirt from the floor of the canoe. A lump formed in my throat as I looked at it, sodden and stained. "I'll look for footprints along the shore."

Russ snorted a laugh. "Come on, Zane, what did she do, swim back in ice-cold water then build a fire on the beach to warm herself and dry her clothes? What happened is she dumped the canoe and drowned. Now let's get to work and find what we came out here for."

Zane's eyes glazed in disapproval, and he turned back to the lake once more as if asking it whether Sarah's corpse was really out there. I wondered the same thing, because as impossible as it seemed, my instincts told me Sarah was not dead. For one thing, the white shirt Russ now tossed casually into the trees was the one I'd made her cover as we fled through the woods two nights earlier. How had it floated to the surface of the lake from *under* her turtleneck?

I was given a Pepsi in lieu of breakfast and told it was time to begin the search for Pete's hiding place in earnest. The exterior of the cabin was primitive in its simplicity, the property empty of other structures. We walked the perimeter in wider and wider circles, looking for anything that indicated buried objects. The ground looked all the same: flat, sandy, and strewn with pine needles.

"We'll have to dig up the yard," Russ said.

"With what?" I knew it was a mistake as soon as I said it.

Russ's face turned a deep red and his eyes bulged. "With your hands if I say so! We're not leaving until we find my stuff. I already waited three years for this." He seemed dangerously close to losing it, and I stepped back, out of his reach.

"We should have something to eat," Zane said.

Wow—a whole sentence! The man was becoming a regular chatterbox, but I guessed he was trying to calm Russ down. Grudgingly, Russ agreed.

Of course lunch was beans. Zane cut up the last two hot dogs and dumped them in. I was pretty hungry, the Pepsi having long ago bubbled along its way, and I noticed the economy-sized "secret recipe" can was almost empty once we'd been served. Was that something to be happy about, or should I worry?

We ate in silence, me sitting on a rock and Russ and Zane standing along the water's edge. I surveyed the property, thinking about where I'd have hidden a large box if I were Pete. I pictured the shoreline as Ben and I had seen it from our canoe. There was nothing but swamp on either side of the cabin. An old logging road led away from the back side, almost obscured by time and probably close to impassable this early in spring. It no doubt led to another, slightly more traveled two-track, which led to a gravel road. I couldn't think of any inhabited houses for at least two miles.

Houses. "The outhouse," I said, unaware I'd spoken aloud.

Russ got it immediately. "Damn, she's right," he said to Zane. "Who'd ever look in a shithouse?" I pictured the frown of annoyance his language would have gotten from Sarah before her practiced serenity settled in again.

After that things were anti-climactic. Once Zane forced open the unused lid of the privy, the goods were in plain sight. Well, actually they were stowed in a trunk and wrapped in several tarps, but it was all there. Pete had resorted to the age-old practice of outhouse tipping, pushing the small shack over on its side. Then he'd made a pallet of firewood and set the trunk on top. Tipping the outhouse back into place hid the goods completely. He'd fastened the cover over the hole, so even if the privy was actually used, that side was inaccessible. Pete was a clever guy, just not clever enough to stay alive with a rodent for a partner.

Russ spent twenty minutes looking through their haul, gloating over each piece. Zane watched stoically as Russ did a running commentary.

"This one came from that house with the purple shutters,

remember that?" Zane nodded. "That one was the British Lady." Russ took out a piece of metal sculpture that would be called an *objet d'art* in some fancy gallery but looked to me like a child had made it. "This was the gas company guy."

Russ' gaze lit on the African piece, and he took it up, handling it carefully. "This was the gas man too, right?"

The piece looked heavy. The base was a solid chunk of mahogany, and springing from its border was a lacy screen of carved figures, dancing around it in scenes depicting hunting, battle, and conquest. It was undoubtedly the item described in the newspaper article, which meant it had a hidden drawer somewhere with a diamond necklace inside. I wondered who else in our little circle knew what I knew.

"This one's kinda tacky, but I like it," Russ commented casually. I wondered if his nonchalance was real or his acting ability had come to the fore. He set the carving aside as if it didn't matter and picked up the next article, a painting that might have been by Dali. Zane couldn't resist a comment. "That was Debbie the census taker."

"Right." Russ laughed at the joke.

I couldn't stand it. "Who are those people?"

Russ smirked at my ignorance. "Those people, dear lady, were all me."

I must have looked as flabbergasted as I was. "You?"

Zane rose as if to say there'd been enough chatter. "I'd better get going."

Russ quit grinning. "Going where?"

"That trunk won't fit in a canoe. I'll trade one of them for a boat."

Russ' eyes narrowed, but the grin remained. "Okay, Zane. That's a good idea."

When Zane spoke again, there was a firmness in his voice I hadn't heard before. "I'll take both canoes." I almost smiled. Zane didn't trust his partner not to cross him!

Russ didn't argue. "Whatever you say, buddy."

"I'll bring the other canoe back with the boat. We need room for four people plus the stuff. Got that?"

Russ turned to me, his grin even oilier than before. "Apparently Zane means to pick up our third partner. He wants to make sure I don't stiff anybody."

I couldn't resist. "Because of what happened to Pete?"

Zane's eyes moved to me with what might have been approval. "I'll lock her up so she won't bother you while I'm gone." Taking that to mean Zane didn't want Russ murdering me in his absence, I took it as a hopeful sign.

In ten minutes or less, I was back in my not-so-luxurious bedroom and Zane, not a deep thinker but certainly a self-starter, was on his way. The second canoe floated lightly behind the one he propelled like he was born to it. As I peered through the shutter slat, the sleek craft looked tiny with his huge shoulders blossoming from its core. I felt like I'd lost my protector.

Though I was afraid he would, Russ didn't come near me. I waited silently all afternoon in the small bedroom, cold but not freezing, scared but not terrified. For a while Russ must have slept, but then I heard him moving around. The outside door closed, and I went to the shutter again to see what he was up to. He moved into my range of vision briefly as he passed, heading toward the crate of stolen goods.

Russ was after the African statue. The fact that he hadn't mentioned it told me that Zane didn't know about the necklace inside it. Russ had heard the story on the news, and that was what had started the new push to find Pete's hiding place. Would he take the necklace and run before Zane returned? If that was his plan, would he kill me before he left so I couldn't tell Zane what he'd done?

My eyes filled with tears. Sarah was my only hope for getting out of this place alive, but how much hope was there?

I had to admit the possibility that my instincts were wrong and she had really drowned. If alive, she could wander the woods for hours and never find a road or a human being, and if she did find the way out, she could leave the area as she'd originally intended. Would Sarah leave me in Russ' clutches, since she'd already done so much to hurt me? Would a friend do that?

But that was it. Sarah was no longer my friend. In her mind we'd gone from friends to bitter enemies. Glancing in the dusty mirror, I wiped my face with my sleeve. It would do no good to get weepy now. I was on my own.

Chapter Twenty-six

I returned to peering out the slit of window left to me. Russ came back into my view, a small, soft bag in his hand of the sort jewelers use to protect fine pieces. It had to be the necklace.

A few minutes later I heard him enter the cabin, and I went still with dread. Now that he had what he wanted, he might decide to eliminate the only witness to his double-dealing, and Zane wasn't around to stop him.

Nothing happened, and eventually my breathing returned to normal. I lay down on my hard bed and waited. After a long time, I heard faint sounds: the scrape of a boat's bow on the sandy beach, the metallic clunk as weight shifted and people stepped ashore. Abruptly the door to my room opened, and Russ stuck his head in. "I'm going to let you out, but if you say one thing I don't like, I'm gonna kill you very, very slowly. Nobody needs to know nothing they don't know already, so just keep your mouth shut."

Steps sounded at the front of the cabin, and the grin I despised formed on Russ' face.

"Great," he called in a jovial tone. "You brought groceries."

"I heard there was a party here," said a female voice. I was only a little surprised that I recognized it. Who else could have been the remaining partner?

"Who's watching the boys?" I heard Russ ask.

"My mom." Angie gave him a hug before turning to take in the cabin. "Yup, this place is as much of a dump as I remembered, maybe more."

When she saw me standing in the doorway, Angie's drawn-on eyebrows wrinkled. "What's she doing here?"

"She's the one that wrote the book," Russ interjected before I could say anything. His frown warned we'd be leaving out further details. Was he too proud to admit he'd once had two prisoners, or was Angie not to know another death had been added to the tally?

Angie frowned, not completely satisfied, but she busied herself spreading the kitchen table with the contents of a KFC bag she'd carried in: chicken, sides, and biscuits. Finishing the spread with a stack of napkins, she stood back like a proud housewife.

As Russ filled a plate, I made some deductions. Angie, a mystery reader, had read *Murder on a Vacant Property*. After I'd unwittingly jogged her memory at the clinic, she'd told Russ about the book's plot and the existence of the cabin.

That had brought the two men to Abaletta. Because Sarah claimed authorship of the book and was a hairdresser, they'd gone after her first. No wonder Sarah had grumbled about the "stupid" novel.

Russ piled his a plate high with some of everything and moved to the couch, where he attacked a drumstick with gusto. Angie and Zane had apparently eaten earlier.

"Go ahead," Russ told me around a mouthful of biscuit. "Eat."

A stronger woman might have refused on principle, but I was ravenous. I justified the generous helping of chicken, potatoes, and coleslaw I took with the thought I'd need my strength if I got the chance to escape.

As I poured slightly cold gravy on the mashed potatoes, thoughts circled my brain like flies that tease but never land. What did I know that could be used to save my life?

Angie sat at the table with me as I ate, her lacquered nails tapping against her Diet Pepsi can. "Why'd you call me?"

I felt my mouth twist in irony. "Believe it or not, I was going to ask if you knew anything about some thefts a few years back."

Her bright red lips curled with humor. "I might." That

seemed to be all there was to say on the subject at the moment.

"How are Tim and Tom?" I'll admit it was a blatant attempt to make her less willing to let Russ kill me.

Her response was perfectly natural, as if we'd met in the coffee shop. "They're fine. They always go right back at it."

"Like their Uncle Pete," I said meaningfully. A glare from Russ reminded me of his warning.

Angie's gaze swung to mine, and something flickered there. Fears she had never allowed herself to examine showed, dark thoughts that were probably becoming harder to ignore. The plot of my book wasn't exactly like their situation, but it suggested a scenario Angie would not want to consider. "Yeah, like Pete."

"What happened to him, anyway?"

Russ stirred suddenly. "Pete got shot by some idiot hunter who shouldna been allowed to own a gun." His eyes met mine, and the message was clear. "I was in Florida, or I would have hunted the guy down and taught him to be more careful with firearms."

Florida, my foot! Russ had sneaked back and killed his partner, expecting that Angie would know the location of the stolen goods. Maybe Pete had intended to cheat his confederates, or maybe he'd been exercising caution. Maybe he had objected to Russ as Angie's boyfriend. Russ wasn't about to tell the truth of it, but it didn't matter. Pete was dead, and Russ was responsible.

"Angie, go out and help Zane repack the crate." Russ' tone was peremptory, almost aggressive. "We need to take off early in the morning."

Angie's face tensed at being ordered around, but she went. As soon as she'd closed the back door, Russ pointed an accusing finger at me, his face hard. "I warned you," he growled. "Things can get lots worse for you."

I tried to look defiant, but my fear probably showed. I was helpless, isolated, and useless now that these people had what they wanted. The best I could hope for was a quick bullet. The other possibilities Russ might devise left me wishing I'd skipped the second piece of extra-crispy chicken.

Angie returned in a few minutes with the silent Zane trailing behind her. "The boat's loaded and ready to go. If we take off at first light, we'll be back in Petoskey by noon."

Russ nodded satisfaction. "One more night in paradise." The glance he gave me caused a chill at the base of my neck.

With the agenda settled, the atmosphere lightened

somewhat. Angie went out of her way to be charming to her man, no doubt a lifetime habit for her. She'd brought a large bottle of Absolut, Russ' drink of choice, and after a few belts, his grin went a little loose. His eyes followed Angie as she moved about the room.

Interestingly, I noticed that Zane's did too. His face was as expressionless as always, but the muscles surrounding the eyes, not as easy to control as other facial muscles, reveal longing in ways that aren't easily definable. If I hadn't been paying attention, Zane would have seemed impervious to Angie's charms as he sipped a lukewarm Bud Lite. But he wasn't.

The conversation turned to their greatest accomplishment, which was finally going to turn a profit. Though Pete had been the one with connections for fencing the goods, Russ claimed he'd met a guy who could "handle things." As alcohol made him more talkative, the one-time child actor explained for my benefit his return to acting.

"I was just a cash cow for my parents from the time I was five." He spoke with the wide gestures common to drunks. "After my mom and dad split, my old lady had a new guy in practically every week. I was acting on the set and acting at home too. Whatever people wanted I could do: a tough guy with kids at school who said actors were sissies, a poor, lost soul with a teacher or a judge who wondered why I broke the rules, or Opie with some schmuck who wanted to be good ol' Andy Griffith. My talent got me out of sticky situations."

"He's great at impersonations," Angie told me, her eyes wide. "He does Paul McCartney and you'd think it was him."

"The detective I talked to said no one had access to all of the houses that were robbed."

"That's how we confused them. Cops don't know everything." One of Russ' brows rose in disdain.

Angie was more than willing to expand on that. "Russ was a lot of different people."

I began to understand. No one person connected the robberies, but a series of seemingly innocuous characters had shown up with legitimate reasons to enter the homes: a census taker, a door-to-door evangelist, a utilities inspector. The owners probably forgot such visitors as soon as they left. Months later, they might not even have remembered to tell the police about them.

"So you went in to look the places over?"

"I even took pictures with one of them little cameras," Russ said proudly. "Pete pointed out items he could sell easy, and I went back during the winter. Zane checked for alarms while he did the landscaping, windows that were easy to jimmy, things like that."

"It helps a lot to know what you're going into," Angie explained helpfully, as if teaching Burglary-for-Dummies.

"Whose idea was it to start with?" I asked. *Keep them talking, make them comfortable with you, let them relax.*

Russ sat back with a pleased expression. "Mine. I met Pete at one of those big Polish weddings where everybody gets drunk and dances a lot. Neither him or me danced, so we sat and talked all night. Pete bragged about how he knew antiques and had all kinds of contacts. That got me thinking."

"So you went to see him later."

"Right. Zane and me had worked together on a job I got fired from, a lawn care business out of Petoskey. We knew that some places in Bay View would be easy to break into. We figured if somebody got inside during the summer and looked things over, we'd know exactly which ones to hit."

"Nobody would find out about it for a long time afterward," Angie put in, "so we'd have time to sell the stuff."

"You gotta get in there and look," Russ said pedantically, "Some of them places just have secondhand junk they should pay somebody to haul away. But other times, people don't even realize what they've got, and there's no security to speak of. People like that deserve to get robbed."

A convenient rationale.

"So you went back to acting, but in a different way."

Russ nodded. "All it takes is makeup, clothes, and stuff."

"That's where I came in," Angie said proudly. "I got my certificate, even if I don't practice."

"You're a beautician?" Again, better that Sarah wasn't here. She'd have been aghast that one of her sisterhood used her powers for the Dark Side.

My mind went in that direction for a moment. Was Sarah, dead, still walking, or hiding in some dark hole? It was cold tonight, but at least it wasn't raining. The white shirt led me to believe she was alive, and I found myself hoping she'd make it to safety, even if she didn't send help for me. As she'd said, someone had to protect Spring.

Angie's reply brought me back to the conversation. "I'm a cosmetologist," she corrected, "but the chemicals made me break out, so I quit and got my real estate license. Now that Pete's gone, I also run the Bar None."

And dabble in criminal activities, I thought, feeling sorry for the twins. No wonder they were so wild.

Sipping at his drink, Russ continued the story. "I started simple, an electric company employee checking up on his meter readers." He switched to a nasal, whiny voice, 'Some of those guys don't really read the meters, so we got to check up on 'em.' Then I tried characters that were tougher to do."

"Like the church lady!" Angie said.

He smiled. "She was fun." His voice rose to primness and his words became clipped. "Mrs. Borden was old, British, and so sweet she'd rot your molars. She had a very weak bladder and always had to use the bathroom."

I'd gotten pulled in. "Why's that?"

"It's on the main floor and usually has a window. Bad old Mrs. B would unlatch it. People tend to forget to check the bathroom windows when they leave."

"Ingenious."

"If there was no wife, we sent in Debbie the census taker. She's kind of a flirt." Russ actually batted his eyelashes.

"Tell her about old Joe," Angie urged.

Russ shoved his empty glass at her, and she rose to refill it. "Bay View is empty in the winter, but they got guys that patrol the place on snowmobiles. We needed someone who could wander around without raising suspicion, someone they were used to seeing. Old Joe was that guy."

"I heard about him from Detective Oskar."

"When the security guys saw the tracks of Joe's snowshoes up there, they didn't think twice about it."

"He sounds like a person who would make it harder for you to move into Bay View and steal things."

"If he'd been himself that winter." Russ's grin widened. "But Old Joe turned out to be me."

Chapter Twenty-seven

Angie explained Russ' comment as she mixed him another vodka and tonic. "Russ went to visit this Joe guy, to see if he might want in on our deal. The poor man had died, right in his own back yard—a heart attack, I guess." She handed Russ the cup. "It was sad, but it was also a big opportunity for us. Instead of calling 9-1-1, Russ put the body in the freezer and took Joe's place."

I frowned. "You moved into the man's house?"

Russ was pleased at my surprise. "Everybody knew *of* Old Joe, but nobody really *knew* him, y'know? There was one of those local color features about him on the local news once. I downloaded it and watched his mannerisms and speech."

"He's amazing." Angie caressed Russ' shoulder. I glanced at Zane, whose gaze had dropped to his beer can.

"As Joe, you were free to wander the area and break into the houses."

"Right. We hoped no one would find stuff missing until spring, but somebody reported a break-in. The police came to question Old Joe—um, me." Russ sat back and stuck his thumbs in his belt, easing the burden of his recent meal.

"And you kept the lights dim so they wouldn't see

through your disguise."

"How'd you know?"

"The detective said that the house was really dark."

Angie sipped at her soda. "That was the end of our run. The disguise wouldn't work if Russ had to leave Joe's house, so we had to let the police find Joe's body."

"You augered a fishing hole and dumped it into the bay."

"That stopped 'em!" Russ crowed. "Joe was their only lead, and he was dead as a mackerel—or whatever fish they catch in Little Traverse Bay!"

The two of them whooped it up at that, and even Zane managed a slight smile. I thought it was more a response to Angie's happiness than to Russ' joke.

It was too great a coincidence to accept that Old Joe had simply died. I guessed he'd been the first, but not the last, victim of Russ Ranett's greed.

Now I saw why Russ hadn't mentioned Sarah and her possible death to Angie. She would draw the line at murder—certainly at the murder of her own brother.

As the trio continued their self-congratulatory reminiscences, I wondered how much Zane knew of the truth. Did he sanction killing off old men and business partners, or had he been left on the edges of Russ' crimes, allowed to participate because he was useful but unaware of the worst items on the agenda? He was a cipher, either too dumb to realize or too greedy to care that he was twice an accessory to murder.

Russ looked at me and his jaw tensed, as if he read my thoughts. Trying to appear more interested than judgmental I asked, "So you spent the winter playing Old Joe."

Angie's her eyes shone with pride. "I'm good with makeup." *If you like it applied with a roller.* "We did bushy eyebrows, the bulgy nose, and lots of blood vessels running across his cheeks."

Russ savored the memory of his greatest acting job. "I walked with a kind of roll, because the old guy had a bad hip."

She giggled. "I swear you'd have thought Russ was eighty."

"I did what people expected from him, ate delivery pizza and bought a bottle of cheap rum every few days."

I couldn't help being curious about the details. "Where was the real Russ supposed to be all winter?"

"He took a layoff from his job and went to stay with a friend in Florida," Angie said. "At least that's what everybody thought."

"I did go down there eventually," Russ said. "That's where I was when Pete got shot." His eyes warned me not to argue that lie.

"I can't believe you got away with all those thefts."

Russ sneered. "You don't believe I could pull it off?"

"It's hard to believe someone didn't see through at least one of the disguises."

"People see what they expect to see, Russ says." Angie finished her drink and set the can aside.

"Right," Russ agreed. "If you're a rich SOB and someone knocks on the door and says she's the Avon Lady, you think, 'How quaint,' and let her in." His grin grew wider as he pointed at me. "And if someone says she's an officer from the Michigan State Police, you tell her what she wants to know."

My eyes widened. "It was you at James' trailer!"

"Bing-O!" He was pleased to have proven his point.

The feeling of having met him before now made sense. "What were you doing at his place?"

"Young Mr. Leigh bragged at the bar that his mother had inside knowledge of some robberies, and that helped her write the book. Miz Leigh insisted that wasn't true. I went to speak to the kid myself."

Sarah, who never told a lie until recently, had spent her life with men who altered the truth to suit their needs. Marv's lie had made her despise me, and James' had made her the target of killers.

The biggest liar of them all, Russ, skipped some important events due to Angie's presence. "Within two minutes of meeting James Leigh I knew he was blowing smoke, but then you came along. I thought about grabbing you when you left, but I'd left the truck on another street."

"Hard to claim to be a state cop when you're driving a beat-up pickup."

"Getting a uniform is easy, but a patrol car?" Russ shrugged. "You claimed you didn't know anything, but there was the call Angie's kid told us about. How did you know she was involved?"

"Angie and I talked about cabins in the area. She reacted oddly when I said I remembered this place."

Angie blushed, but Russ shrugged it off. "You probably would have figured it out anyway once the cops started asking you to remember what Pete said."

"I can't understand why he moved the stuff." Angie

seemed hurt that her brother had held out on her, but I guessed it was her association with Russ that had kept Pete from sharing.

"Lied to his own sister." Russ' ironic glance confirmed for me that he wouldn't have shot Pete if he'd suspected she was in the dark. I glanced at Zane. If he knew Russ had killed Pete, how could he ignore the fact that he'd be a liability once he'd done the heavy work?

Zane merely opened another can of beer.

Our party—the oddest one ever—wound down after that. Some secrets had been revealed, others waited to be told. I'd been treated as an audience because at least one of my hosts was certain I'd soon be dead. When the conversation lagged I said, "I need to use the privy."

"I gotta pee too," Angie offered. "I'll go with her."

"No!" Russ' bark was louder than it needed to be. When we all jumped, he toned it down. "Zane can go. She can't outrun him."

I moved to the battered sink in one corner and put my garbage into one of the plastic bags. Grabbing the forlorn piece of soap there, I stuck it in my pocket, along with a couple of napkins. Zane waited for me at the door, handing me a flashlight as I passed by.

Inside the outhouse, I made the appropriate noises but at the same time worked quickly on my second purpose for being there. Females sit at such moments, and I leaned toward the opposite wall, my piece of soap in hand. It was hard as a rock, but that was good. On the rough wood I traced R KILD P, going over it several times to widen the letters. I hoped they'd show up well enough in a flashlight beam to catch Angie's eye.

As soon as Zane and I returned to the cabin, Angie stood to take her turn. "How bad is it?"

I shrugged a What-can-you-do? answer. She grimaced, took up her own supply of napkins, and left. When she returned minutes later, I watched her carefully. Though her eyes never met mine, Angie was definitely nervous. She fluttered around the room, cleaning up the night's leftovers as if it were vital to leave the place tidy in the morning. I noticed she didn't meet Russ' gaze either, which gave me cause to hope my message had done its work. It would be good if she'd had the presence of mind to scrub it away with her foot before leaving the outhouse.

Finally Russ said, "Ang, leave that and come on. We gotta get some rest." She smiled at him, but her heart wasn't in it. I wondered how he didn't notice.

I was sent to my cell again, and the chair scraped as it slid into place under the doorknob. A few seconds later I heard the back door slam and the sound of digging on the beach. Looking out, I saw Zane burying the remains of our meal. At least he knew enough not to toss it into the woods and possibly attract bears.

The bed was no better than before, hard lumps spread over an even harder wood surface. I lay listening to the conversation in the next room between Angie and Russ.

"Why did you bring her out here?" she asked.

"We needed her to help us find this place." Russ' tone didn't invite further questions.

"And what happens to her now? Do we take her back to the road and let her go, or what?"

"We'll leave her here, so we have time to get away."

"But she'll be okay, right? We can leave her the rest of the chicken and stuff."

"Sure, sure," Russ answered breezily.

"Okay," Angie responded. "I mean, she was always real good to the boys, you know?"

"Yeah. She's a nice lady."

I could have screamed. Could Angie really be that dumb?

If she believed Russ would let me live, she probably didn't believe he'd killed her brother. Some people won't see the truth, no matter how clearly it's set before them.

Once again I tried to form an escape plan. If Angie knew about the diamond necklace, she and Russ might be keeping it from Zane. Or was Angie the one in the dark? Could I live through this if I appealed to one of them for help? Should it be Angie? Zane? It certainly wouldn't be Russ.

Chapter Twenty-eight

I don't know how much I slept, but daylight brought a terrible clatter in the cabin's main room. At first I was confused, but in a few seconds I heard Russ ranting and cursing as well as I've ever heard it done. Everyone has talents, I guess.

After a few minutes, the swearing subsided and the back door slammed. Peering through the shutter I saw Russ and Zane on the lakeshore, staring out over the water. The boat was gone.

Angie had taken off with the goods, probably because of my message. Despite the fact that it didn't help my situation, I had to smile. Russ had lost his loot and his girl, and I'd made it happen.

It was easy to follow the action outside, because Russ was so angry that every word came through loud and clear. "Get her!" he ordered Zane. "She is dead meat!"

Zane didn't answer, not that I expected him to, but the look that passed over his face was interesting. Even some distance away and peering through the slats, I saw that his profile registered objection. To Russ, to Angie, or to what, I had no idea.

Zane hauled the canoe out of the trees and pushed it into

the water. I wondered how much of a start Angie had. Probably not much. She'd have waited for daylight in order to be able to find her way. She was an amateur in a clumsy rowboat with skinny arms and fake fingernails. Zane's huge muscles rippled obediently to his athletic body's commands. Angie didn't have a chance.

"When you catch her, wait at the truck," Russ ordered. "I'll finish here and walk around the shoreline."

Zane took off smoothly and speedily in the canoe, but his paddle hovered over the surface of the water for a moment. "Don't hurt the woman," he called back. "Just leave her here."

"What?" Russ was taken aback, either at Zane's care for me or his issuance of a counter-order.

"Lock her inside. Don't hurt her." Two sentences. *Go, Zane!*

Russ gestured impatiently. "Okay! Okay! Just catch Angie!"

Zane didn't even look back.

"Stupid bitch!" Russ fumed as he watched him go. "I was good to her too."

The tirade went on for some time. Russ had many, many unkind words for his former girlfriend, and it took time for him to calm down. He paced the beach, kicking up sand and throwing odd bits into the water in spite: sticks, rocks, even an empty cooler.

After a while he remembered me. As he looked toward the window I ducked back, though it was unlikely he could see me watching through the tiny crack. He surveyed the cabin as a whole, thought about things for a few seconds, then nodded to himself.

Next I heard him inside the cabin, rummaging around in the main room. From the swish of plastic bags I concluded he was gathering things, probably fashioning a make-shift pack by twisting two grocery bags together and using one handle from each for shoulder straps. He might guess the terrain would be challenging and he'd need his hands free, but he had no idea how tough it was going to be. I had a moment of satisfaction picturing how soon he'd find that out.

I examined the room once more for possible means of escape. Once Russ was gone, I would pound at the window until the shutter gave, climb out, and run in the opposite direction.

A feeling of dread hit, however, as the meaning of new sounds penetrated my consciousness. Paper crackled, and Russ came first to the bedroom door then went outside and moved busily around the cabin. When I heard the clink of kindling from the wood-box piled it against the walls, I got a sinking feeling. There would be no time to make my escape. Russ was preparing to do as he'd threatened earlier: burn me alive.

It wasn't me his mind was focused on, however. "I've got the biggest piece of the haul," he muttered to himself, "But when I find her, she's dead anyway." Fiercely he slammed a piece of wood under the cabin wall.

"Just leave me here!" I called through the door. "By the time I get back to town you'll be long gone."

"You know who we are." Russ spoke calmly, as if I'd understand if he explained correctly. I caught the sulfur-y odor of matches being lit. His voice came and went as he moved about the cabin, lighting several small fires. "That ought to do it," he said finally. "You'll die of the smoke. It won't hurt." That was as kind as Russ Ranett got. He didn't intend my death to hurt.

I didn't wait for him to be out of earshot before I broke the glass with my shoe and began pounding at the shutter. Smoke rose under the door behind me, and outside as well, at the base of the cabin wall. There was no way to get a purchase on the slats, which were so close together I couldn't wedge even a finger between them. I tried yanking on the paneling that covered the old chimney hole, but I knew that was a faint hope. Even if I got it off, there was still the Red Man sign nailed to the exterior wall.

I went back to the window, my best hope. It was too high to get my shoulder into the effort effectively, but I rammed the shutter frantically, coughing between attempts. Five times, seven times I ran across the room, jumping as high as I could and battering clumsily at the shutter. It barely rattled.

Soon I couldn't breathe for smoke, the woody kind that's so nice around a campfire but much less pleasant when the very boards around you are being consumed.

I pulled my shirt over my mouth and nose. How long did the public service spots say you could survive in a room filled with smoke? I tried not to think about it, gathering my strength for another attempt, though my shoulder throbbed from the previous ones. I was unwilling to die without resisting, unwilling to let a creep like Russ be the end of me.

Suddenly the shutter flew open, letting in light, air, and best of all, Zane, big shoulders and all. His huge arms rippled as he twisted one panel off, tossed it to one side, and turned to take a grip on the other one. The hinges gave way with a shriek of protest. As he threw sand on the burning wall below me, I pushed myself through the window, falling heavily onto the beach and then scrambling away from the cabin.

I lay for several seconds on the damp sand, struggling to get fresh air into my smoky, protesting lungs. Without conscious decision I crawled to the lake to splash water on my face and neck. Though mucky and icy cold, it felt good. I think I even drank some.

When I was able to sit up, I turned to look at my former prison. It was a box of flame, and the dry old wood popped and snapped as it was consumed. Zane watched impassively.

"You came back," I croaked.

He cocked his head to one side like a robot trying to compute. "Zane hadn't heard about the necklace." Turning, I saw Angie standing at the water's edge, beside the canoe. She held the African statue between her arm and hip. Gazing at her very silent partner, she added, "The necklace isn't in its little hiding place, and when I told Zane, he decided we should come back and talk to Russ about it."

"I'm very grateful, Zane." I tried to sound like someone whose life had been spared, but it came out merely polite, as if he'd offered me his seat on a crowded bus.

Learning about the necklace must have convinced the somewhat thick-headed Zane that Russ would never play fair with him. Added to that, and maybe more important, was the realization that Russ would kill Angie if he got his hands on her. Zane wanted the necklace, and now he had his chance with Angie as well. Rescuing a middle-aged mystery novelist was probably way down his list, but it meant a lot to me.

"Russ is gone," I began and was proved wrong before the words were out.

"So you did catch her."

We turned to see Russ standing at the tree-line, that stupid gun in one hand and that stupid grin once again on his face. Smoke from the cabin fire drifted between us, and his body seemed to sway in the waves of heat passing through the air.

He glanced at me. "You could have told me it's impossible to get through along the shore."

"Because I'm here to make your life easier?" I asked. I can't help it. Sarcasm comes naturally sometimes.

"It's okay," he assured me. "I have a ride now, right, Zane?"

"You held out on us." Zane's tone was flat. There was no surprise at Russ' duplicity, just an indication of where things were going from here. He and Angie had become "us."

"I held out on her," Russ corrected, pointing at Angie. "She's got no business sharing with us on this. She didn't do nothing. A little makeup, a few trips to the Salvation Army store. She didn't take chances like the rest of us did." He paused. When Zane made no comment, Russ went on to his secondary argument. "Besides, it was her brother that screwed us over in the first place. We'd be long gone if Pete hadn't hid the stuff way out here."

"He knew you too well," Angie said accusingly. "Pete was right not to trust you, and now Zane and me don't trust you neither."

"That's a problem that's easily solved." Russ raised the gun, pointing it at Angie's chest. Everyone froze for a second, or at least it seemed that way to me. The scene etched itself into my brain: Angie's eyes widening in fear, Russ' gloating gaze, and Zane—

Zane was in motion. For once, his face revealed his thoughts: understanding of Russ' intent, fear for Angie, and determination to protect her.

As Russ' hand twitched, there was a pop like a pine knot exploding. Zane crossed in front of Angie just in time to take the bullet in the chest. He continued past her for a few feet then fell onto the sand. His face didn't turn away from the impact as he dropped like a stone. I stared in horror as a splotch of red blossomed from the back of his T-shirt.

With a curse, Russ again turned the gun on Angie, who reacted with speed born of self-preservation, ducking behind the canoe as three shots followed her progress.

I stood there, frozen, but a familiar voice brought me to my senses. "Run, Caroline!"

I obeyed, sort of. My crab-like crawl could hardly be called running, but I realized I could well be Russ' next target.

Sure enough, two shots pinged toward me, but the smoke from the burning cabin obscured the beach, ruining Russ' aim. Pulling myself to temporary safety around the side of the outhouse, I came face-to-face with Sarah.

"What are you doing here?" I stammered. I'd pictured many scenarios: Sarah drowned, Sarah at the sheriff's office urging Damon to hurry to my rescue, and Sarah on the highway flagging down a helpful motorist so she could hop a plane for Rio. I hadn't imagined her here, rescuing me from bullets and death.

She shrugged. "I didn't know where to go, and I didn't want to leave you." She added irrelevantly, "I climbed a tree."

"A tree?" It was odd to converse while Russ plotted how

to kill me.

"You said people look at eye level, and that's what Zane did. He walked right under me." With a weak grin she added, "I almost killed myself getting down out of it. After that I just hung around, trying to figure out what to do. I thought once Zane left I could get you out, but Russ set the cabin on fire. I was coming to help you but then Zane came back."

"They thought you drowned, but I noticed the wrong shirt was floating in the lake."

Now Sarah's grin was genuine, revealing white teeth in a dirty, smoke-smudged face. "No man would notice that." She gestured toward the spot in the woods where Zane had concealed the canoes. "I took both of them and put the other one back."

How like her. If she'd headed out right away, she could have been back with help by now. Instead she'd chosen to wait and worry, and we were no better off than before. Still, it was comforting to have her beside me.

I peeked out at Zane, immobile on the sand. "Is he dead?"

"I don't know." Sarah's tone was matter-of-fact. "If that gun holds six bullets, he's used them all up." She surveyed the beach, zeroing in on Russ' position. "He either has to reload or take the boat and go."

"He plans on no witnesses, and he's got one down already." I'd seen no movement near the canoe. "Maybe two."

"His plans may have to change." Sarah squinted at the lake. "The fire's bound to be seen. It will take a while this far out, but someone will come."

That cheered me somewhat. I'd be happy to help Russ launch the canoe myself if that's what it took for him to leave us alone. Then we heard a scream. Through the smoke I saw Russ haul Angie up by the hair and give her a vicious cuff with the gun butt that sent her sprawling on the sand. I made a little sound of protest, but Sarah's hand on my arm warned me to silence. The fact that he hadn't shot Angie lent credence to Sarah's six-shot theory.

Russ squinted through the smoke for several moments, saw no sign of me, and concluded I'd taken off. It was almost comically easy to read his mind. He considered chasing me, decided it wasn't worth it, and turned away. He scanned the area, wiping his cheek and leaving a smear of soot across his face. Nothing moved but the flames that were making a meal of the old cabin.

Russ approached the inert body of Zane. He searched his pockets fruitlessly, and I heard a low curse. I whispered, "He wants the truck keys. I saw Zane put them in the wheel well, in one of those magnetic boxes."

Poking me, Sarah pointed in the opposite direction. The canoe had floated down the shore and now rested directly in front of us, rocking gently in the shallow waves. "Take it and go," she urged softly.

I looked at her in amazement. "What about you?"

"You'll be lighter and faster alone. Go now!"

Sarah was right. In a canoe I could beat Russ to the boat launch, take the truck, and get help. Since he didn't know Sarah was here, he was no danger to her.

Without further delay I sprinted to the canoe and pushed off as hard as I could, heading toward the bend that would shield me from sight—and from bullets. I kept the paddle upright and my strokes the right length for optimal thrust. Since I didn't dare look back, I had no warning when the first shot zinged over my head. Russ must have reloaded from bullets in his pack. I lowered my head and kept paddling.

I might have made it, but his gloating voice drifted over the water. "Hey, lady, look what I got!" I turned to see him standing over the barely conscious Angie, who had managed to rise to hands and knees but was having trouble with the next move. Russ laid the gun to her head. "Now turn around and come back here or watch me splatter her brains all over the sand."

Chapter Twenty-nine

How did he know I'd obey? Angie was nothing to me, but then again, she was a human being, and while saving me hadn't been her first priority, I'd have been burned black by now without her. Telling myself I had no choice, I turned the canoe. At least Sarah was still hiding nearby. But, the thought arose bleakly, what could she do?

I was back on shore within a few minutes of my departure. Angie shot me a look of gratitude, but neither of us showed much optimism for the future. The cabin still burned fiercely, throwing heat I could feel fifty feet away. It wasn't likely to set anything else afire, since the trees were still wet from the recent rain. A sturdy stick lay near my feet. Could I bend, pick it up, and attack Russ with it before he shot me? Not likely.

"You two have caused me a lot of trouble," Russ growled. "It's time to end it." A pop at my right made us all turn, but it was only the fire. Smoke rose like a black plume, advertising its presence. The DNR would be on the way.

Russ surveyed the canoe nervously, distinctly uneasy with the idea of navigating it himself. Still, he'd tried the shoreline and found how treacherous it was. A canoe was his only escape, despite his fear of it and of the water. Bending, he pushed it out far enough to float it. Like every city slicker I've ever seen, he tried to keep his feet dry in the process, which is usually a wasted effort. He didn't push off far enough, and his weight simply pressed the keel into the sand. With the gun in one hand, Russ was doubly clumsy.

The second time he did better. Setting his pack on the floor of the craft, he checked to see that it was stable then took aim at Angie. We both froze. There was nowhere to run, no escape.

Just before the gun went off, a potato-sized rock flew from the trees, hitting Russ in the knee. It deflected but didn't entirely ruin the shot, and Angie fell to the sand, blood staining her yellow T-shirt.

Russ turned with a roar, but the first missile was followed quickly by another. This one caught him on the collarbone, causing him to lower the gun and grab his chest.

Sarah had apparently been busy, locating several good-sized rocks that fit easily into her hand for throwing. She hadn't played softball for years, but my friend still had a good eye and a natural pitching motion. Her work at that moment was prettier than anything I'd seen her do in high school.

While Russ glared into the trees at his unseen foe, I took

advantage of the distraction, picking up the stick and launching myself at him. I managed a good whack across his arm before he turned back, and the gun fell into the water with a plunk. He stepped toward me and got another rock in the middle of his back, causing him to arch in pain. The next one missed, hitting the water with a splash, but a smaller one followed quickly, bouncing off Russ' temple and bringing a response that was more yelp than roar. He lunged toward the trees, but I stuck the stick out and tripped him. As he went down, I caught him a glancing blow on the arm. My makeshift club broke from the impact, but the new, shorter version was actually more serviceable for close quarters. As he tried to push himself up from the sand, I stepped close and laid it soundly across the back of his evil-stuffed head.

Russ wobbled for a while like a boxer avoiding the count, grabbed at me, then fell, landing on his face in the water. I waited a second in case he was faking, but finally I relented and saved him from drowning.

Sarah emerged from the trees, waded into the water, and picked up the gun, holding it as if it were a snapping turtle. It was a relief to see it in friendly hands, though hers shook so badly I was a little worried about accidental misfire.

"Be careful with that." Wordlessly she handed the gun to

me, and thankfully it came butt first. I'm no gun enthusiast, but I had fired a pistol a few times and knew how to put the safety on. Feeling silly carrying the thing around like one of Charlie's Angels, I tried putting it in the waistband of my pants. Does anyone ever admit the lump that makes is uncomfortable and feels ridiculous? Glancing at Russ to make sure he was motionless, I laid it on the seat of the canoe.

"Is she all right?"

I went to Angie, splayed on the sand like a forgotten toy. Though Russ' bullet had only grazed her arm, she lay with eyes closed, unresponsive.

I splashed cold water on the gunshot wound, which didn't look serious. "Breathing's normal. Pupils look okay."

"Good." Sarah looked around. "We need to find some rope and tie Russ up."

"Zane has a pocket knife. We can cut the leader off the canoe." We moved up the beach to where Zane had fallen. I felt his carotid. He was dead, though the heat of the cabin fire had kept his skin warm. I felt creepy going through his pockets, but the knife was there.

Sarah gave a shout of warning, and I turned to the beach and saw Russ paddling away in the canoe. Though his movements were awkward, he had it going in the direction he wanted. He looked back once, a sneer distorting his features, but other than that he concentrated on putting as much distance between him and us as possible.

I muttered a word no lady should. For once Sarah didn't frown but nodded agreement.

Russ was going to get away. Worse, the gun was in the canoe. Would he simply take his chance and escape, or would he try to get revenge on the two of us?

The answer came swiftly. Russ turned, and I saw his hand rise. Sarah and I dropped to the ground in synchronized panic, and the bullet that followed a second later sped into the trees behind us. Flat on my stomach on the wet sand, I looked into Sarah's eyes, which were as wide with fear as I imagined my own to be.

After a few seconds I raised my head slightly. One shot seemed to have satisfied Russ, and he concentrated on paddling. He did pretty well for a while, but as he got to the deep part of the lake, he made two mistakes almost every novice has experienced.

When you paddle a canoe, your hands tend to squeeze as you push the oar through the water then relax as you pull it forward for the next stroke. However, if you don't pick the paddle up high enough, the blade strikes the water while your grip is loose. Before you know it, the paddle is behind you, floating on the water.

That was Russ' first mistake.

The second mistake was worse. When the paddle left his hands, Russ should have used his hands to drag the canoe to a stop then guide it backward. Instead, he disobeyed the only command I'd ever given him. Neither sitting straight nor holding still, he leaned out and back, trying to reach the paddle. His lunge tipped the craft farther than it could tolerate, and it slid gracefully over into the black water.

Russ made almost no protest. His arms flailed briefly, but the shock of the cold and his fear of water must have paralyzed him. In seconds he was gone, drowned in the icy waters of the lake.

It took a while for us to comprehend the events of the last few minutes. Two men were dead. Angie was hurt, how badly I didn't know. Sarah and I were safe. There was sure to be help on the way, though our rescuers had no idea what they would find. The cabin still crackled behind us, and billows of smoke blew past every few seconds, obscuring the still water before us.

I checked Angie again. She looked terrible: a huge knot

rose over her right eye, and tracks of mascara ran down her face, making her resemble an avant-garde painting. Her vitals were good, however, and the wound on her arm had stopped bleeding by itself. I wasn't sure why she was unconscious, but self-preservation might have been part of it. The body protects itself in interesting ways when it's traumatized.

"She seems okay physically," I told Sarah, "but she's in a lot of legal trouble. With twin boys to raise too."

"That's not right." As always, anything that would hurt a child wasn't right in Sarah's book. Considering the situation as a whole, I had to agree. Angie wasn't the brightest, wasn't the best of mothers, wasn't even very honest. But she'd been unaware of Russ' worst crimes, and she'd lost a brother because of him. She loved her boys, and she'd returned to save me. The diamond necklace probably figured in there somewhere, but nobody's perfect.

"We'll tell them how she came back for us. I'm sure they'll give her a break."

"You tell them." Sarah avoided my gaze. "I'm leaving." There was challenge in her voice.

"Leaving?" I echoed dimly. "Where can you go?"

"You won't see me again."

"But Sarah—"

Cool blue eyes turned to mine, and I saw a mute plea along with firm determination. There was also a hint of our old friendship. "I probably knew Marv was lying. I just wanted so much for you to not be right one time. For you to do the wrong thing."

I understood but couldn't agree. "I always thought you were the perfect one. So many lemons in your life, and you always made lemonade."

She smiled, and her eyes softened. "We made a pretty good team, didn't we?"

I looked away. Sarah wanted me to let her run away from everything she'd done. My first thought was she couldn't make it without someone to lean on. "How will you live?"

"I have the advance money. And I can do hair anywhere." She added in an unaccustomed tone of irony, "Especially the way I do it." Putting out a hand as if to forestall my next argument, she added, "I'll figure out a way to let them know you wrote the book. You'll get the rest of the money."

"It isn't about the book, Sarah. Not anymore."

"No, it isn't," she agreed. "It's about Spring. I'm taking her with me." Her voice turned fierce. "Don't you see? I'm the only chance that child has. If I go to jail—" She didn't finish, didn't need to. If Sarah stayed in Abaletta and faced her crimes, she'd be charged with crimes. In all likelihood she'd be treated lightly because of her blameless past, but in the end, she'd be deemed unfit to raise a little girl, even if she summoned the courage to accuse her own son of child abuse.

You can blame me if you want to, but I was thinking of three kids who needed parenting more than The System needed a questionable sort of justice. I allowed someone who'd made my life miserable for two years to walk away without a word of blame. And I decided right then I'd lie to the police about Angie too. I'd claim she had no idea what Russ, Zane, and her brother had been up to.

When I gave a nod of understanding, Sarah turned immediately and walked off into the woods. Maybe she had nothing more to say to me, maybe she didn't trust herself to say it, or maybe she wanted to be gone before I changed my mind. She faded from sight at almost the same moment the first wail of a siren sounded, still miles away. It was the last time I ever saw her.

Chapter Thirty

Six months later I got a weird email. I don't usually open them if I don't recognize the sender, but this one was titled Burning Your Cabins Behind You. That intrigued me, and I couldn't resist.

As I waited for my computer to download the attached photo, I looked at the pile of stuff on my desk. There was a letter from my publisher, finalizing deadlines for my second book. Thoughts of "my publisher" and "my book" gave me a thrill, but I was beginning to grasp the reality of it too, the demands on my time, the work of promoting, and the niggling little negatives that displaying creative work brings: petty jealousy, well-meant criticism, and snobbish dismissal of work that's not "literary" enough for some. Still, it was exciting, and I'd enjoyed it so far.

A few friends insisted they knew Sarah didn't write the book, but the consensus was she'd been her usual sweet self when she submitted it for me, like the famous author's wife who kept writing to agents for him when he'd given up in frustration. Everyone assumed she'd intended to make an announcement any day about who was really responsible. Sarah's reputation is even stronger these days, and everyone speaks of her as if she qualifies for sainthood, which involves being perfect and being dead.

I let them.

I recalled the scene at the lake as if in a dream. Fire trucks first, then police cars, one of them spilling out a tearful Rachel, who had arrived to find me gone and been frantic with worry. She calmed down after she'd assured herself I was all right, and by the time I was allowed to leave she suggested, with that tilt to her eyebrow that means she's plotting, that I ride back to town with the sheriff.

While I appreciated my daughter's efforts on my behalf, I couldn't help wondering how Damon could be attracted to a malodorous woman with sand, mud, and myriad other bits of nature clinging to every square inch of her. I must say, though, he was gallant and even a bit chatty on the trip, at least for Damon.

I turned the reward for finding the diamond necklace over to the sheriff's department. In the first place, two deputies had to dive to the mucky bottom of that lake to retrieve it, and all I did was point to the general area. In the second place, Damon Bates had faith in me when others didn't, so I owed him.

Everyone was kind about my vagueness concerning the

experience, assuming the trauma I'd gone through made me unsure of the details of my kidnapping. Of course there was the bump on my head too. The accepted version of the story has Russ and Zane drowning Sarah and Spring in an attempt to make them tell where the loot was hidden. Angie had been an unwitting dupe, wounded and almost killed trying to save my life.

Marv and James Leigh muddle on, becoming more and more alike in both looks and drinking patterns. Few people in town feel sorry for them anymore, but that's okay. They do pretty well at that on their own.

One day after things had settled down, I drove out to the Bar-None Bar. I surprised the proprietor, not being the type of customer he usually sees, but I said I used to know Angie. He told me she'd sold him the place on a land contract and moved to California. After we chatted a while, he confided the cause had been her boyfriend, who'd drowned trying to steal some stuff.

"Her boyfriend was a thief?"

"I guess he was a real bada-a-a—" He remembered his manners just in time. "—bad one. Killed some people, according to the papers."

"And Angie, was she in on it?"

"No. It came out the boyfriend killed her brother, who owned this place before she did. After all that, I guess she wanted to get away from here."

"I'll bet she did," I commented, trying to keep any ironic inflection out of my voice.

***

When the picture finally loaded, I stared at it for some time. The subject is a little girl in a park. She wears a dress of blue with a hat to match and soft leather shoes. It looks like she's been to church, and I picture someone suggesting a leisurely lunch and a walk in the park afterward.

The city is unidentifiable. The park could be any of ten thousand, domestic or foreign. The child laughs as some ducks crowd around her, fighting for bread crusts she's strewn on the grass. There is no text, but I knew right away that the child, and the woman behind the camera at whom she smiles in perfect trust, are not only safe, they are happy.

Other Books by Peg Herring

The Simon & Elizabeth Mysteries: Tudor Era Historical

Her Highness' First Murder

Poison, Your Grace

The Lady Flirts with Death

Her Majesty's Mischief

The Loser Mysteries: contemporary-homeless sleuth

Killing Silence

Killing Memories

Killing Despair

The Dead Detective Mysteries: mildly paranormal

The Dead Detective Agency

Dead for the Money

Dead for the Show

Dead to Get Ready—and Go (2016 release)

Writing as Maggie Pill

The Sleuth Sisters Mysteries

The Sleuth Sisters

3 Sleuths, 3 Dogs, 1 Murder

Murder in the Boonies

Peg Herring lives in northern Lower Michigan, where she reads, writes, and loves mysteries. She and her husband enjoy travel and gardening, two great pastimes that don't coexist well. Peg also writes as her younger, hipper alter ego, Maggie Pill.

Peg's website: http://pegherring.com
Maggie's website: http://maggiepill.maggiepillmysteries.com/